Submerging

SWANS LANDING #2

SHANA NORRIS

ISBN-13: 978-0-9884509-9-8

Many waters cannot quench love;
rivers cannot wash it away.

- Song of Songs 8:7 (NIV)

Chapter 1

Land had disappeared from view over three weeks ago. Newfoundland had been our last stop, the last time my feet had touched sand.

The last time either of us actually had feet.

The Atlantic Ocean stretched on in every direction, endless undulating waves of gray-green. Fog hung thick in the orange and purple dawn sky, so it was impossible to tell whether I really could see shapes on the horizon or if it was my own wishful thinking.

My body had grown tired of swimming. It ached deep within the bones with the need for land, for sand under my toes. It ached to have toes again instead of the red scaled tail I'd had for much of the past two months. I was finfolk and fully amphibious, able to move between land and water whenever I wanted.

"Are you sure we haven't ended up in Africa?" I asked my half-brother Josh Canavan. His head bobbed

1

among the waves next to me.

"I'm sure," he said.

"But how do you know?" Nearby a bird swooped low to investigate us. Squawking, it flew away once it saw we weren't fish. "Maybe we got turned around somewhere and have been swimming in the wrong direction ever since. Maybe that's Swans Landing ahead of us now."

Sometimes I suspected Josh wouldn't mind if we were on our way back to the island where we'd grown up along North Carolina's Outer Banks. I knew the only thing he wanted was to see Mara again. The few times he slept, drifting on the ocean's surface, he murmured her name while he dreamed.

Mara Westray had walked into my life three months earlier and had taken everything away from me. My grandmother, my best friend, my brother. She'd stolen them all one by one with that naive act. She could play the poor girl with the dead mama thing well, I had to give her credit for that. It had blinded everyone, except me. I wasn't going to pity her for anything.

Besides, having a dead mama didn't make her any more of a special snowflake than anyone else was. My daddy was dead and my mama had left when I was a baby. Yet I didn't see anyone falling all over me like they did her.

Josh smirked, squinting in the sunlight reflecting off the water. "You don't live up to your name much, do you?"

I scowled. *Sailor.* The ridiculous name my mama had given me before she'd disappeared from my life. "What's that supposed to mean?"

"Sailors usually have a good sense of direction based on celestial objects," Josh said.

I hated when he started talking like a huge know-it-all. Which he was. He tried to hide it, but the guy was practically a genius. He just knew things; about events, objects, and even people. Things you didn't want him to know. It was like he could sense them.

Josh pointed toward the sky, where the sun was beginning to peek through the fog. "The sun," he said. "During the daylight hours, we can base our direction on it. It's the easiest to remember. The sun rises in the east and sets in the west." He traced an imaginary line across the sky, from one horizon to the other.

He nodded in the direction we'd been traveling before we paused to rest. "The sun is rising ahead of us, so we can logically assume we're traveling east."

I made a face, rolling my eyes. "Okay, brainiac. What about at night? There's no sun to follow then."

"We can follow the stars. If you know what constellations to look for and their position in the sky this time of year, you can easily figure out what direction is east."

That was exactly what I meant by "practically a genius." He had always looked tough in the halls of Swans Landing School, hiding in his giant black hoodie and walking around with a permanent scowl on his face, but underneath, the guy was a total geek. It was something most people didn't know about him.

Of course, there was a lot that people didn't know about him, such as the fact that he was finfolk like me. Josh had perfected the art of living a double life.

"Some of us have better things to do with our time

than to stare at the sky all day and night," I told him. I laid back in the water, stretching my arms out to my sides. Flicking my red tail fin, I splashed an arc of salty spray toward Josh.

He barely blinked when the water hit his face. He laid back too, letting his silver tail fin flick lazily among the small waves.

"Besides," Josh said in a quieter tone, "I can feel the land calling me. Can't you?"

I let out a long, slow breath, letting my mind go blank. Water gurgled in my ears as I bounced on the surface.

Yes, I could feel it. A tug deep within, pulling me toward the mists to the east. It was an urge stronger than anything I had felt before. Finfolk belonged to both land and sea, and so we could feel the essences— what we called songs—of both within us. The thing that made us able to change form also tied us to life along the coastlines. Our bodies constantly fought between the urge to walk on land or swim in the ocean.

"I feel it," I told him.

"Then we'll keep swimming," Josh said, and I knew he was as hungry for the shore as I was.

The longest swim of our lives had begun two months ago, as best as I could tell. It was hard to keep track of time. We had traveled up the North American coast, following a path we hoped would lead us to the ancestral home of the finfolk. Since then, it had been nothing but a long, endless swim across the Northern Atlantic. Normal humans wouldn't have been able to make it this long without help.

But the two of us had never been normal, nor

entirely human. Being finfolk and fully amphibious allowed us to breathe underwater and swim with the ease of dolphins.

At first, I had been happy to be submerged in the water for so long. I had lived most of my life on land, pretending at being human like most of the other people on the island. It was hard sometimes, resisting the strong call of the ocean constantly beckoning me in. I could understand why my mother had left when I was only a few months old, why she decided not to fight the urge to disappear into the water. There was only so much a person could take before resisting felt pointless.

But the curse of finfolk was that we never belonged wholly to sea or land. And after a few days at sea, my body began to crave land again. I could see the same longing in Josh's dark eyes, though he never spoke about it.

"We must be getting close to the finfolk homeland," Josh said. "I've never felt the ocean's song this strongly before."

All we knew was that the finfolk ancestral home was somewhere off the coast of the Orkney Islands in Northern Scotland. Or at least, that was what the myths said. No one we knew of had ever seen it. Our people had left Scotland generations ago and had lived in Swans Landing for three hundred years. Some finfolk had left Swans Landing over the recent years in search of our old homeland, but no one had ever returned. We didn't know if anyone had found it.

We didn't know if it even existed at all.

But it was the only way I could hope to find out

what happened to my mama. I had to know why she left and what happened the night Josh's and my daddy died.

Thinking of Swans Landing always caused an ache in my chest. I thought about my Grandma, the woman who'd raised me after my mother left. She didn't want me to go on this trip. Grandma always had excuses to keep me from leaving. If it were up to her, I'd live and die on that island.

I splashed water in my face to hide the tear that trickled down my cheek. Grandma would be okay without me. She had Mara now, a replacement granddaughter, she didn't need me.

"Ship," Josh murmured next to me.

I rolled over, looking in the direction he pointed. On the horizon, a dark spot moved closer, slowly growing larger.

The trick to swimming across an ocean was to avoid being seen. Two teenagers swimming far from shore couldn't be easily explained. It wasn't too difficult once we'd left land behind, but there were still the occasional freight ships passing by or planes flying low enough overhead to see us.

"Let's go under," Josh said.

He dove into the water with grace, as if he'd been living in it his entire life. Actually, Josh hadn't known he was finfolk until he was nine years old. He'd been playing on the old broken pier back home and had fallen in. Lucky for him, I'd been there, swimming without Grandma's permission. I'd seen him fall and had gone to save him. I'd known even then that Josh was my half-brother, though he didn't. His mother had never told him about me or about the fact that his father was descended from finfolk.

Or that our daddy had died because he fell in love with my mama.

Josh had changed and became finfolk for the first time that day long ago, and I'd been the only one who had known. I'd kept his secret for years, teaching him about our people.

I followed Josh deep under the surface. We couldn't go as far down as some ocean creatures, but we could go deeper than normal humans could without scuba gear. The ocean wasn't as murky this far from land and so we could see some distance in front of us. Schools of fish swam by underneath and jellyfish glowed iridescent as they passed.

Josh darted in front of me, leaving behind a trail of bubbles, and I hurried after him. We couldn't speak underwater, so we had to surface for anything more than hand gestures. During our weeks of swimming, the two of us had become good at knowing what the other was thinking. A quick glance was usually enough to convey thoughts.

So when Josh stopped suddenly, his face grim, I knew the icy trickle up my spine was a reflection of his thoughts even though I hadn't yet seen what he had.

I swam to his side. *What's wrong?* My eyes asked the unspoken question.

Josh nodded to an area ahead of us and I turned to scan the water. A dark shape sliced through the shadows ahead, darker than the rest of the area under the ocean's surface. Around us, fish suddenly darted, swimming away and leaving an eruption of bubbles behind them.

I didn't know a lot about the ocean outside of Swans Landing, but I did know enough to realize that when the other sea life got out of the area, it was a bad sign. A very bad sign.

Josh pointed up, but I shook my head. We couldn't surface. The boat would have drawn closer now, since it was moving toward us and we were swimming toward it. But the dark shape still loomed ahead, growing larger with each second.

"We're finfolk," I tried to speak even though I knew speaking underwater was useless. A fountain of bubbles escaped from my lips, drowning out my words.

Josh gave me a puzzled look and I made elaborate hand gestures, trying to indicate that we should keep swimming. We were as much a part of the sea as anything else here was, and we had the advantage of being fast. Both of us were in good shape and finfolk could swim nearly as fast as dolphins when they needed to.

But Josh didn't look convinced. He gestured toward the surface again.

Sometimes I couldn't believe the two of us shared the same father. He could be cautious and timid, while I wasn't the kind of person who sat around waiting for things to pass. I took action. I'd led us out here on this trip across the Atlantic and I wasn't going to let anything stand in my way.

Turning an expert flip, I spun around and darted ahead, leaving Josh still gesturing toward the surface. I didn't look back to see if he was following, but I knew he would. Josh was one of those guys, the kind who felt like he had to look after the people he cared about. He would never let me go off toward some unknown danger all on my own.

So I wasn't surprised a moment later when I felt him at my side. He tried to grab my arm, but I dove deeper into the water, my arm slipping from his fingers. I'd had a lot more swimming experience than Josh had and the water was a part of me. I could move with little effort, slicing ahead through the darkness.

A startled eel slithered out of my way as I passed and I watched over my shoulder as it twisted in half-circles behind me. Josh barely noticed the eel as he swam after me, his silvery tail flashing as it caught sunlight that broke through the water.

Josh stopped suddenly, his eyes widening. I twisted around to see what had him so panicked.

A wall of wriggling, silvery fish swept toward me, moving through the water so fast I didn't have time to respond. I became swept up in the wave of bodies around me, fish bumping and biting against my flesh as they panicked, trying to get away.

I swam down, fighting against the mass, pushing through scales and sharp teeth. Just as I could see the edge of the mass, I crashed hard into something rough that refused to give way.

A net. The boat we'd seen above hadn't been a freighter, it was a fishing boat.

Chapter 2

Josh grabbed my arm, trying to pull me through the mass of fish as the net closed in, darkening the water around me. I tried to fight my way through, but I didn't get far before I was snatched back.

I twisted around, trying to peer through the mass of wriggling fish to see what had me trapped. A loose rope from the net had wrapped itself around my tail fin. I pulled at the water-logged rope while slapping fish away from my face.

Josh grabbed onto the rope and pulled to try to break it free from the net, but the rope was too thick. He swam back to me and grabbed my arm.

For a moment, I thought maybe everything would be okay. The rope would come loose or the weight of the fish would break through the net.

But my arm was wrenched from Josh's as the net lurched toward the surface. The fish around me struggled harder, bumping and bruising my body all over. Josh swam after us, looking up at me with wide, helpless eyes.

We had come so far, so long and so close, and now I was doomed to being caught in a net like a fish.

I opened my mouth, bubbles erupting into vicious streams as I tried to call out to Josh. The net broke the surface of the water, sending the weight of the thousands of fish down onto me. I gasped as the air was pushed out of me and I wriggled to free myself from the crushing mass on my back.

There was always a moment between being finfolk and being human when I felt not fully whole. As if my body was torn between two different forms and couldn't decide which it wanted to be.

Usually, the change back into human form after being finfolk was pretty easy. It was a lot less painful than changing from human to finfolk, since the scales along my legs were sliding back into my skin rather than slicing through on their way out. My bones still popped and distorted as my tail fin divided itself back into legs once again, but it was easier somehow.

But this time, the process felt agonizingly slow as the net moved on a giant crank toward the boat's deck. "Come on, come on," I chanted to myself. Whether it was the mass of wriggling, panicked fish all around me or my own palpitating heartbeat, the change took a lot longer than it should have and I began to worry that the men on the boat would soon discover a mermaid in their net.

"Whoa!" a voice shouted. "What's that in the net there?"

"Come on!" I chanted again as my thighs split apart.

A group of men gathered on the deck, leaning over the rail look at me as the net hung suspended over the water.

"Is that a person?" someone asked. "A body?"

"Get her out of there! Call the doctor!"

The last of my red and silver scales slipped under my skin, leaving only faint pink marks where they had disappeared and I was once again human. Half-naked, but human.

I had seen fishing boats back home bring in their catch and I knew they usually didn't take much care in being gentle with the fish. They'd let a whole load of fish dump onto the deck into a huge, sliding mass. But this time, the net was carefully lowered toward the deck inch by inch, until finally my back pressed against the wood of the ship and the net around me slackened, releasing the fish in a slithering wave.

I laid for a minute on the deck, my body still and my eyes facing up toward the sky. The rope still lay twisted around my feet.

"Is she dead?" someone asked.

I could feel the men all around me, peering down at my limp form, half-covered in fish that gasped for breath outside of the water. I felt a pitying kinship with these fish, having been snatched unwillingly from the ocean in the same net and for a moment, I imagined myself scooping them up and throwing them overboard to freedom.

"Aye, likely dead," said another voice. "Why else would she be out this far?"

I blinked away the salt water in my eyes and then

sat up, causing a few of the men to jump and gasp.

"Um," I said, looking at the grizzled faces that stared back at me. "Hi."

The men stood in stunned silence for a long moment, gaping at me.

"What were you doing in the ocean, wee hen?" asked one of the older men, his beard gray and thick, Grandpa-like.

"Oh..." I said, drawing out the word as I tried to think of an answer that wouldn't cause any alarm. A shipwreck wouldn't work, they'd call the Scottish equivalent of the Coast Guard to report it. No wrecks of any kind. Which left one answer I could give.

"I was, you know, going for a swim," I said, smiling wide at my rescuers.

The six men exchanged looks, raising their eyebrows. For a moment, the only sound was the slapping of the fish as they flopped on the deck and the water lapping at the sides of the boat.

"Do you...eh..." The gray haired Grandpa-like man gestured toward me, his cheeks reddening. "...usually swim half-clothed? So far from shore?"

The one inconvenience to being finfolk was that I couldn't wear clothing on my lower body. If a finfolk changed form while wearing jeans, they would be ripped to tatters, unusable once he or she had changed back into human form. Sure, I could have worn a skirt and been okay, but they had a habit of twisting and bunching up around my waist while I was swimming. They were too annoying for long periods in the water.

"Oh, right," I said, looking down at my legs, which were bronzed from a lifetime outdoors. "The current pulled my clothes off."

"The current?" the man asked.

The boat rocked and I reached out to steady myself on a large wooden crate. "It's pretty rough out there. I don't recommend going swimming today." I pulled the waterproof bag off my back and unzipped the biggest pocket. "I have some more clothes with me."

The men were decent enough to turn away while I dressed. I wasn't exactly shy, but I appreciated their gesture. Finfolk quickly got used to being half-naked in front of other people.

Once I had pulled on a slightly damp pair of jeans— the waterproof bag wasn't as waterproof as it claimed to be—someone draped a thick woolen blanket over my shoulders for warmth. It was early May, but the air here was much colder than the warm May days I was used to. The water that dripped from my hair and soaked through my shirt was icy.

I scanned the water's surface quickly. I hoped Josh wouldn't try to board the boat to save me. It was hard enough to explain my presence. It would be impossible to explain why *two* of us were wandering around the ocean half-naked.

"Care for a cuppa?" the gray haired man asked. "It isn't good, but it's hot."

I shook my head. "No, thank you. Actually, I should be getting back." I made a movement toward the side of the boat, but the man lurched forward, grabbing my wrist. He stared at me with wide eyes above round cheeks pink from the cold air.

"Are you mad?" he asked. "That water is freezing. You can't possibly think of swimming back to shore."

I couldn't explain to him that finfolk could handle colder water temperatures than humans could. And I couldn't explain that my half-brother was waiting in the water for me to return.

"Maybe she's a mermaid, Malloy," one of the other men said, laughing. "She has to get back to her own people, you know."

The men laughed and I forced myself to laugh with them. *Don't look nervous,* I told myself. These men obviously didn't believe in stories about mermaids. They had no reason to believe I was anything other than an insane girl who took frigid swims too far offshore.

But still, the gray-haired man called Malloy eyed me with a curious look. "Why don't you have a seat in the cabin," he said, smiling kindly. "Get out of this wind. We'll take you back to the harbor."

My gaze darted toward the water. All that stood between me and freedom was a deck covered with glistening, flopping fish, gasping their last breaths. What would the men do if I suddenly ran for the side and jumped overboard? Would they call the police? Would they send divers after me?

"Don't attract attention," Grandma had always told me. Tourists visited Swans Landing during the summer and the way we kept ourselves safe was to keep our secret and remain invisible in front of outsiders.

Sorry, Josh, I said silently as I squeezed my eyes shut and let out a long breath. Then I opened them and smiled at Malloy.

"Thank you," I said through clenched teeth. "That

would be nice."

I let Malloy lead me into the small cabin of the boat, hoping Josh would be smart enough to stay out of sight until we reached land.

Chapter 3

The fishing boat pulled into the harbor as the sun sank in the west behind us. I'd had to stay on the boat while the men took in their catch for the day. They were polite and courteous, and I didn't feel too out of place aboard a fishing boat. I'd spent my life growing up near, on, and in the water. My best friend Dylan Waverly and I had helped Lake Westray reel in crab pots and rake for oysters in the Pamlico Sound. The water was my life.

I kept watch at the bow of the boat, my hands gripping the rails as the land approached. The day had never warmed up much and I shivered in the strong breeze that swirled around me. My eyes scanned the water constantly for signs of Josh, but he was nowhere near the surface, which left me both relieved and worried.

Malloy, the captain of the ship, had warned me

several times that I might get seasick, being so close to the front of the boat. But I never got seasick. It wasn't something that happened to finfolk.

"Where are we?" I asked as the other men rushed around, tossing ropes and climbing overboard to the creaky dock below. A city lay clustered around the shores of the harbor, sloping among the hills that stretched out behind it.

Malloy eyed me, raising one bushy gray eyebrow. "You're a long way from home, aren't you?" He'd kept his eye on me ever since I'd arrived on the boat. Goosebumps prickled along my spine whenever I caught him staring at me with a look like he knew I was more than what I seemed to be.

When I didn't respond, he said, "We're in Stromness. On the Mainland. Orkney."

Orkney! So we had at least made it to the right area.

"I'm here visiting family and got a little lost while swimming," I said, trying to keep my voice calm. "Maybe you can help me. Do you know of anyone by the name of Mooring?"

Malloy scratched his head. "Mooring? No, can't say as I do. I know many families here in Stromness, but no Moorings."

Finding the finfolk and my mother wouldn't be easy. There had to be a clue, something I could go on that would lead me to the next step from here. Josh's last name wouldn't be much help. Canavan was purely a human name. His finfolk genes came from his great-grandmother.

When I asked if he knew any Waverlys, Malloy shook his head no. I pushed aside thoughts of Dylan and focused on other finfolk family names I knew. I ran through a short list—most of us were related to each other and shared the same last names—but Malloy didn't have any leads.

"What about...Westray?" I asked, cringing as I thought of the girl who had stolen Dylan's heart.

Now Malloy narrowed his eyes. "Westray," he repeated, rolling the word out in his thick Scottish brogue. "Can't say as I know anyone here named Westray, but there is an island by that name."

Tingles shot their way across my scalp like tiny spiders. "Where is this island?"

Malloy nodded into the distance. "North of the mainland." He gave me directions from Stromness to Kirkwall, where there were ferries that traveled to the islands farther north. He rubbed his thick beard with one hand. "Only, I don't know what you'd hope to find. The village there is even smaller than Stromness. Not much to interest a wee hen like yourself."

His gaze burned into my skin, seeping deep into my bones. I swallowed, keeping my hands clenched on the railing to hide the trembling. I knew not all humans were friendly toward finfolk. I had grown up with warnings of what some of them might do to us if they found out our secret. As kids, Dylan and I used to try to scare each other with stories of finfolk ending up as aquarium exhibits. Not that we'd ever heard of that actually happening, but it was a recurring nightmare we'd both had once.

I felt like I should say something, anything to distract us from the current conversation. But then Malloy spoke again.

"Well, what should I do with you?" he asked. "I would probably be in trouble if I let a lassie I plucked out of the ocean go wandering off without evidence of a passport to prove you're here legally."

I hadn't thought of this problem. Of course I didn't have a passport. I didn't need one during a swim across the Atlantic Ocean.

I opened my mouth to speak as a shout echoed across the dock. "Sailor! There you are!"

Josh stood on the wooden deck, his hands on his hips. He was dressed in only slightly damp jeans and a black hoodie, his bag slung across his back.

"Your boyfriend?" Malloy guessed.

I rolled my eyes. "Worse. My brother. Is that proof enough that I'm here legally? I have family waiting for me."

Malloy studied me for a moment, but then he nodded. "Aye, go on to your family."

I giggled, trying to sound light and carefree, like a silly American girl who had gotten lost while swimming in a foreign country. "Thanks for the ride."

Malloy walked me over to the rusty metal ramp where I could descend to the dock. "My pleasure. But next time, better keep to swimming near the shore."

Josh stood like a glowering statue as I made my way down the dock toward him. Only when I had reached his side did he move, wrapping one thick hand around my arm and pulling me away from the boats and the people as quickly as possible.

Josh didn't say anything as we maneuvered away from the docks and into narrow streets between small shops.

After a moment, I'd had enough of Josh's silent glare. "Say what you want to say," I told him.

A muscle in Josh's jaw twitched. "You could have been killed," he said. "Or *found out.*"

"I changed back to human form before they got a good look," I said. "Besides, I doubt any of them would have believed they'd really caught a mermaid if they had seen anything. They probably would have brushed it off as a trick of the light or something." I waved a hand dismissively.

"This isn't Swans Landing, Sailor," Josh spat at me. "We have to be careful. We don't know how the people here would react to finfolk."

I pulled my arm from his grasp, snorting. "Right, because the people back home were *so* friendly."

Not everyone in Swans Landing was finfolk. In fact, most of the people on the small, isolated island were human. The locals all knew our secret, but the only reason they didn't reveal us to the rest of the world was because no one else would believe them. Still, relations between finfolk and humans were not pleasant—due to the fact that I had been born.

The humans in Swans Landing blamed the finfolk for the death of Josh's and my father. They blamed my mother for seducing him and tempting him away from his human wife.

All my life, I'd lived with the knowledge that my very presence was the reason for the tension among the people of the island. Lake, Mara's dad, insisted it was the declining fishing industry and the strained economy causing many of the problems, but I knew better. I had seen the way some of the people looked at me. I knew what they thought when they saw me.

It was good that I had left.

"Did you happen to find out where we are while you got a ride to shore?" Josh asked, interrupting my thoughts.

"I did," I said smugly. "We're in Stromness." I stopped and turned to him, feeling my heartbeat quicken with excitement. "We made it to Orkney, Josh. We're here. Now we just have to find the rest of the finfolk."

"And how exactly do we do that?" he asked. "I don't think they advertise their location."

"The captain of the ship told me about an island to the north. It's called Westray."

I cringed at the light in Josh's eyes and the quiver of his lips. I knew the name would make him think of Mara. I hated that she could have such a strong effect on him from thousands of miles away.

"That's where we have to go," Josh said, nodding to himself as if he had a sudden insight. A moment before, he'd had no direction, and now, because of some stupid girl back home that he barely knew, he had everything all figured out. "We'll find what we're looking for there."

Chapter 4

I had spent a lifetime on ferries. Swans Landing was accessible by only two ways: private boat, or a three hour ferry ride that ran three times each day, beginning at 7 A.M. and ending at 7 P.M. each night.

When I was little, leaving the island with Grandma was an adventure. I'd always stand at the front of the boat and watch the water foam as the ferry sliced through the current. Seagulls hovered around, waiting for me to feed them a snack from the bag of chips I'd beg Grandma to buy from the galley.

Somewhere along the way, the ferry ride lost the magical quality it had once held. I stopped going to the mainland except for a handful of times over the last four years. My body rebelled at being too far inland anyway, leaving me feeling light-headed, nauseous, and craving salt water.

Yet, the ferry ride from Kirkwall to Rapness Pier in

Westray had left me invigorated. The air was charged with something I had never felt before. Everything felt different, older and more alive.

When we arrived in the village of Pierowall, Josh pulled his cell phone out of his pocket again and glared at it. "Still no signal," he said. He had insisted on bringing his cell phone with him during the trip, wrapping it up in three plastic sandwich bags inside the waterproof bag to make sure it didn't get wet.

A few people milled through the village, men nodding to us as they passed and women giving a warm smile. Children eyed us curiously, obviously noting that we were outsiders. It was odd to be an outsider. I had spent so much of my life within the confines of Swans Landing, seeing the same people every day.

"I think we're probably far outside your service area," I said.

I led the way into a gray building marked "Hostel." A desk was set in the front lobby of the hostel, covered with scattered papers and a phone. It looked busy, but there was no one in sight.

Josh peered up the stairs as if someone would magically appear because he wanted them to.

I tapped the little silver bell on the desk several times. The ding echoed through the room. I kept slapping it until the sound became so irritating that no one would be able to ignore it.

"Coming!" a female voice called from a room off to the left. A moment later, a young woman bustled through the door, holding a laundry basket propped on one hip. She deposited the basket on top of a stack of papers on the desk and then moved behind it to look at us.

"May I help you?" Her gaze flickered between us, before settling on me, as if she knew I'd been the one ringing the bell.

"We need a room," I said.

"Do you have a reservation?" she asked.

I raised my eyebrows. "Do we look like we'd have a reservation?"

"I have a bunk room available," she told us. "How long will you be staying?"

Josh and I exchanged a look. "Is it possible to stay on a night-to-night basis?" he asked.

She looked at us again for a long moment before answering. "Checkout time is at noon each day. If you haven't checked out by then, you'll be charged for another night."

We'd exchanged some of our money to pounds before we'd left Stromness, so Josh handed over enough cash to cover the first night. Our room turned out to be barely bigger than a closet and contained a set of twin-sized bunk beds.

"I get the top," I said as soon as I spotted the beds.

Josh scowled. "Thanks for letting me have a chance to consider."

I shrugged. "I'd be too afraid of you crashing down on me to ever sleep."

Josh let out a grouchy huffing noise, then tossed his bag onto the lower bunk.

"I saw a general store across the street," he said. "We should go buy some food before it closes."

I wasn't in the mood to go out again. I was hungry,

but I was also desperate for some solitude. I'd been stuck with Josh attached to my side for two months. I needed a moment to breathe and think without hearing his voice.

"I'll wait here." I climbed into the upper bunk and stretched out. I hated to think of how many other people—greasy, sweaty people—had laid on this same bed. But it was a bed and it didn't rock and it wasn't wet. I probably would have laid on a mattress stuffed with hay and proclaimed it to be the best thing I'd ever felt right about then.

Josh crossed his arms. "We should be careful."

"I am being careful," I said. "I'm waiting here while you go to the store."

But Josh didn't make any movement to leave. I could see him debating whether to go or to keep fighting with me.

"I'll be right here when you get back," I told him. "The longer you wait, the longer it's going to be before we can eat and the more irritable I'll be when you finally get back."

"Fine. But don't go anywhere. Don't touch anything. Don't speak to anyone. Got it?"

I waved my hand again and closed my eyes. "Got it, big brother. Now go."

I breathed a sigh of relief when he finally disappeared through the door. Usually I hated being alone. Being alone gave me too much time to think. But right then, I relished the solitude. It was nice to not have to talk to anyone or keep up appearances about what anyone else expected me to feel or say or do.

To not have to pretend I wasn't homesick.

What time was it back in Swans Landing? Did Grandma miss me? Did Dylan? Did anyone even wonder if I was okay or still alive?

Grandma and I had argued the morning that I left. The memory flooded my thoughts.

"You've always kept me from finding my mama," I had shouted at her. "It's your fault I'm still stuck here. And it's probably your fault she left in the first place."

Grandma's eyes had flashed with anger. "You watch your mouth, Sailor Mooring. You don't know what you're talking about. I've done *everything* I could for you all these years to make up for your mama leaving."

"But you're *not* my mother," I had told her. "I want to find her."

Grandma had shaken her head. "You go after her and all you'll find is heartache. No good will come if you follow in her footsteps."

But I'd had to go. I had left with only a change of clothes and a few food items stuffed into the rubber bag I'd bought the year before in preparation for the trip. My first instinct had been to go to Dylan and beg him to leave with me.

But Dylan had been angry at me for keeping secrets from him about Josh and Mara. So instead, I had gone to Josh and he had agreed to come with me.

A gentle shake woke me and I blinked, my vision blurry. "Sailor," Josh said softly. "Wake up."

I groaned, rubbing at my eyes. I had been dreaming about being back home in Swans Landing. Grandma was scolding me for having done something, though I didn't know what. She chased me around with her wooden spoon, threatening to pop my bottom, which she had been threatening to do since I was two years old but had never once actually followed through on.

Then Dylan was there and we escaped to the ocean, swimming as far as we could. It was like it had always been meant to be, just the two of us.

Until a whale crashed through the water, swallowing Dylan whole and leaving me behind.

"What did you get?" I asked as I pushed the remnants of the dream out of my mind. I slid off the bunk to the floor to inspect the bags Josh had.

"Peanut butter and bread," Josh answered. "I thought this might save us some money, since we have limited funds. Water. Crackers."

"No chocolate?" I growled.

Josh reached into a bag and pulled out a few candy bars.

We ate in silence for a while. Despite the fact that I didn't care for peanut butter sandwiches, it seemed like one of the best meals I had eaten. At least it wasn't seaweed or raw fish, which was what we had been living on for the past two months.

"It's getting late," Josh said. "We should go to bed and then we'll explore the village tomorrow."

"We've been swimming for weeks without rest," I said. "I'm planning to sleep for days."

After we ate, I headed to the bathroom to try to wash up. I had never been a girl who spent hours on her looks. I kept my straight brown hair long because it was an easy style. I never wore makeup. It washed off whenever I was in the water anyway. But still, I was shocked at how tired and dirty I looked when I saw my reflection in the tiny bathroom mirror. My face was gaunt, my cheekbones almost cutting through my skin. My hair was dry and brittle from months of saltwater. Did this happen to every finfolk who spent so much time at sea, or was it a result of the weakened human part of me?

I didn't have a comb, so I ran my fingers through my hair in an attempt to unknot the strands. The saltwater had turned it into tangled waves around my shoulders.

After washing my face and rinsing my dry mouth with water from the squeaky faucet, I returned to our room.

"Bathroom's all yours," I said, climbing back into my bunk. While Josh disappeared into the bathroom, I laid across the bed once again. Already I could feel the pull of the ocean wanting me back, but I'd had enough of the water to last me a lifetime. For now, I wanted to sleep on dry land.

I drifted off to sleep before Josh had returned.

Chapter 5

I opened my eyes to a white ceiling only inches above my face. My body ached and my muscles seared with pain as I rolled over. All of that swimming had toned my arms and legs, but it had also worn them completely out. I didn't think I'd be able to walk properly for the next month.

Leaning over the side of the bunk, I saw Josh was still asleep, his arms thrown over his head and his mouth open in a snore. Somehow I had managed to sleep through the noise. I must have been more exhausted than I thought.

I slipped out of bed carefully to keep from waking him. I was not in the mood to deal with his bossiness yet.

It was early, judging from the pale sunlight streaming through the windows, but I wasn't the only one up. Some other guests wandered between their rooms and the bathroom, and in the kitchen I found the woman from the front desk making coffee. My stomach growled at the smell.

"Good morning," she greeted me with a quick nod. "There's hot coffee and tea if you'd like. And you can have use of the stove if you need to cook anything."

Thanks to Josh's peanut butter and bread, my cooking options were limited.

"Thanks," I said, padding over to the counter to pour a small cup of coffee. I liked mine loaded with sugar, so much that Grandma always called it "coffee-flavored sugar water." When the woman turned her back, I grabbed a nearby saltshaker and added a few shakes in as well. The finfolk genes made me crave salt constantly whenever I wasn't in the water.

I stood near the window as I sipped my coffee, looking out at the semi-circle bay. The fog was thick on the horizon, but I could see the shape of land across the water.

"What's that island out there?" I asked casually. "The one across the water?"

For a moment, I hoped she would tell me no island existed there. I'd read once in a book about finfolk that they were known to live on vanishing islands. Maybe this was one of them, and my journey to find the finfolk was almost over.

"That's Papay—Papa Westray. It's only a short trip over if you want to tour it."

I wasn't really interested in the tourist thing, but I did need to explore Westray at least. Keeping up the appearance of an American tourist, I asked, "Are there tours here, around Pierowall? Or around Westray itself?"

The lady nodded. "There are some, but if you ask me, you don't need to wait for a tour. You can easily walk the island at your own pace."

I drank the last of my coffee and thanked her.

A quick visit to our room showed that Josh was still asleep. I was unable to remain still, a feeling of restlessness sweeping over me. I glanced at Josh once more, biting my lip. A quick walk wouldn't hurt and I'd probably be back before he woke anyway.

The morning was cold and my breath hung in the damp air. Gray clouds filled the sky, but other people were out and about along the main road. It was a small village, much like Swans Landing, and the people all seemed to know each other, judging from the way they smiled and waved as they passed. I had journeyed thousands of miles to end up in another isolated island.

Did any of these people ever feel suffocated, stuck here on this island with the same people they had known all their lives? Back in Swans Landing, it was impossible to hide or to blend in and be invisible. All of your problems were known by everyone else and secrets were hard to keep hidden.

My chest tightened, as if it were being constricted by an invisible hand. I needed to get away from people, from the small town enclosure I was in once again. I needed wide open spaces, room to breathe.

I stumbled down the street, trying to keep the panic off my face as I gasped for air. I brushed by people, sometimes knocking into them, but I didn't stop. My feet moved faster until I was running past shops and homes.

Finally I broke free of civilization. Wide, green fields spread out around me. I kept walking for a long time without any destination in mind. The wind whipped my hair around my head, the strands stinging my face.

A white lighthouse grew larger in the distance the farther I walked. My gaze focused on it and my feet moved faster toward the structure.

The Swans Landing Lighthouse had always stood watch over me throughout my life. It wasn't a tall lighthouse, short and stout, but it was bright white with a single black line around its middle. This lighthouse on Westray was much taller, but it was also white, and for a moment I could almost imagine myself being exactly where I had started from.

The lighthouse was surrounded by a low wall and I wasn't sure if I would be trespassing if I got close to it, so instead I strolled across the open field around it toward the edge of the cliff on which it stood.

Swans Landing always felt like the edge of the world since no other land was visible from its shores. But this felt like the other side, like the water stretched on forever. The land dropped out before me, falling into cliffs high over the ocean. Waves crashed against rocks far below and all around me hundreds, maybe thousands, of seabirds swooped and dove from their perches along the exposed rock.

I sucked in the deepest breath I could, breathing the familiar salt air. I stood on the opposite side of the Atlantic Ocean that I had always known, but still it was the same. I knew the sound of its song and the taste of its salt in the air. I was home.

The earth had a song of its own, though it wasn't sung as often as the water songs were. It was older, quieter, and harder to hear over the sound of water. But here it felt stronger, the vibrations more intense than I'd ever felt them before.

I closed my eyes, breathing the sweet air deep into my lungs. The songs of the earth below my feet and the water farther down competed inside me for attention. They merged for the briefest moment into one sweet, ancient song, unlike anything I'd ever heard before. It dissolved quickly, and the two songs were once again separate. I pressed my lips together and hummed along with the familiar water song.

"Sailor," a voice whispered around me. When I opened my eyes, I saw her dancing along the cliff in front of me. My song faltered and she started to dissolve into golden bursts, but then I continued humming and her image grew vibrant again.

My mama, young and beautiful, wove her way around the field, smiling and throwing her head back to laugh. She looked happy, the way I always imagined she must have been when my daddy was alive, when they were in love. Had she been happy when she realized she was pregnant with me, even though my father was married to another woman? Had she loved me because I was a part of him?

I choked back a sob, the song faltering, and my mother faded away, dissolving into a golden mist. It was the human part of me that let me see her when I heard a finfolk song. It was the human part that made me weak.

I feel to my knees in the grass, burying my face in

my hands and letting the wind take away the sound of my crying.

"Singing in public is not the best idea around these parts," said a voice thick with a Scottish brogue behind me.

My head snapped up. A guy not much older than me stood in the grass, chewing a long green blade between his teeth. His bright blue shirt stood out against his pale skin and red hair fluttered in the breeze.

My first instinct was to run. But where? He stood between me and the rest of civilization back in Pierowall.

Besides, he had already heard my song. Every muscle in my body was tensed, ready to fight if needed.

"Who are you?" I asked.

"Callum Murchadh," he said, nodding at me. "And now may I ask, who are you and where did you come from? You do not belong here."

A chill tickled down my spine. "What makes you say that?"

Callum shrugged. "Not hard to tell. I know everyone in Pierowall. And I know the kinds of people who usually come here on holiday." His gaze scanned over me. "But you are no tourist."

"I don't know what you're talking about." I stood and brushed grass off my knees. "I have to go."

I walked past him, but Callum reached out and grabbed my arm.

"I heard you sing."

I froze, panic tickling its way up my spine and across my scalp like tiny spiders. "So?" I asked, pulling my arm from his grasp.

He shrugged again, looking out toward the water. "So it was a nice song."

I studied him for a long moment, trying to determine who he was. *What* he was. He looked human, but then, so did I.

"Who are you?" I asked.

He rubbed his cheek, cocking his head to the side. "I think the question is, who are you?"

"I'm...a tourist," I said, but my voice sounded small and pathetic, not at all as confident and tough as I wanted it to be.

He laughed and the sun shone on his brilliant red hair as he moved his head back. "And I'm just someone who lives by the water."

He walked closer to the edge of the cliff, looking over as if deciding whether to jump off.

"Did you follow me here?" I asked. There was no one else around. Would anyone hear me if I screamed?

Callum gazed out at the water as he spoke, his hands in his pockets. "If anything, you are intruding on me. I've come here every morning for the last five years. I think I have the right to ask where you came from."

He was tall and his clothes hugged his body in that perfect way they should. He stood so that the sun outlined his profile, showing off the strong curve of his nose and chin.

"My brother is waiting for me. I should go." I wanted him to know I wasn't here alone, in case he turned out to be psycho. A good-looking psycho.

"You can stay if you'd like. But you should know

that people can hear you."

"Well, that's good," I said. "Because if you come near me, I'll scream."

"So who are you?" he asked again.

I shook my head, crossing my arms. "I'm not stupid. I've seen plenty of horror movies. I won't be the gullible girl that gets herself killed by the charming foreign guy."

He smiled, revealing gleaming white teeth and a deep dimple in his left cheek. "I'm charming, aye, but harmless."

I snorted. "Why should I take your word for it?"

"Because," he said, "you could easily get away from me. If you ran, I would be at a disadvantage." He reached down and pulled up one leg of his jeans, revealing a metal artificial leg. He tapped it with one finger. "It gets me around, but slows me down a wee bit. I've never been much of a runner anyway."

My mouth opened and closed for a moment as I tried to think of an appropriate response.

He let his jeans leg fall back into place. "You don't find me quite so charming now, do you?" he asked, his forehead creasing into a scowl. "Don't look so pityingly."

He turned toward the water, breathing in deep. The wind rustled the grass around us and birds shrieked over the ocean.

"I love the salt air, don't you?" he asked.

I didn't answer as I stared into the hazy distance.

"I've lived all my life near the water," Callum went on. "Almost a part of it, you could say. I never get tired of it."

My gaze practically bored holes into his skin as I studied him for any clues as to who he really was. But he looked like any other human boy, though not quite a boy. He was probably a couple years older than me, still pretty young-looking, but with shoulders that had broadened nicely.

"What about you?" he asked. "Do you have a love affair with the ocean too?" He winked one brilliant green eye my way.

I sighed. "Sailor. My name is Sailor, okay? Can you leave me alone now?"

"Sailor. The girl from the ocean. I'll remember that."

The hairs along my arms stood on end. "I'm not from the ocean. I came on a ferry, like normal people do."

"Aye, keep your story straight and maybe people will believe it."

Callum moved toward me and I tensed, my body poised to run if needed. Why had I never bothered to learn a martial art? How did I expect to protect myself from cute psychos who may or may not know what I was?

"A bit of advice," he said. "It might be best to keep your songs to yourself in the future."

Then he passed by without stopping, heading back down the road toward the village.

Chapter 6

"Where the hell were you?"

Pushing my hair out of my face, I looked up at Josh, who stood outside the hostel door. His hands were buried deep in the front pocket of his hoodie and his expression was stony, his eyes dark with fury.

He looked like a big brother, all protective and fierce, and I felt like I was being scolded for coming home too late from a date.

"I went for a walk," I said as I brushed by him.

Josh grabbed my arm and spun me around to look at him. "You've been gone for hours! Do you know how worried I've been since I woke up and found you missing? Fiona said she had no idea where you'd gone, you were here one minute and the next—"

"Wait a minute," I said, holding up my hands and brushing off his grip on my arm. "Who's Fiona?"

He blinked for a moment. "Fiona." He gestured at

the door of the hostel. "The woman who runs the front desk. Fiona McIntyre."

"So you're on a first name basis with her now? What, did the two of you get all cozy while you were supposedly so worried about me?"

Josh shot me a dark glare. "I had time to talk with her while I was waiting on you to get back from wherever you'd wandered off to."

I smirked. "I'll bet Mara would be interested in hearing all about your new friendship with this Fiona."

I'd meant it as a joke—Fiona had to be at least twenty years older than us—but Josh's eyes flashed and his nostrils flared. He was too sensitive when it came to Mara Westray.

"Mind your own damn business, Sailor," he growled. Josh stomped through the door of the hostel without waiting to see if I would follow.

The woman, apparently Josh's new best friend Fiona, stood behind the desk sorting papers. She raised her eyebrows when we entered.

"There she is," she drawled, eying me up and down. "Your brother had a right good fit waiting on you."

"Well, now he's being a right good ass," I snapped.

Josh glared at me and then stomped toward our room. I took that as my invitation to follow. Once in our room, Josh unfolded a map he'd bought at the general store and studied it.

I sat down in the chair next to the window. I tried not to think about Callum and what had happened at the lighthouse, but the harder I tried not to think about it, the more I did. Should I tell Josh that this guy might know what we were? A gnawing feeling in my stomach warned me that I couldn't brush him off.

"So," I said, clearing my throat, "what's the plan?" I was chickening out, but I didn't want to have that conversation with Josh right now.

Josh didn't look up from the map. "We need to look for clues."

"What kind of clues?" If I was lucky, we could leave this place behind before Callum spilled our secret to all his friends in the village.

"I don't know," Josh said. "This was your idea. Didn't you come up with a plan for once you got here in all those years you thought about this?"

My plan had always been to find my mother. I'd never considered the work involved in getting to that point. I'd certainly never imagined months of swimming across an ocean.

I'd always focused on the reunion between my mom and me. I'd thought about how she might look and what all the other finfolk she lived with were like. What would happen once I made it to Scotland hadn't crossed my mind.

"Well?" Josh asked.

"We should go swimming tonight," I said. "We'll see if we can find something that will lead us to the finfolk homeland. A door, or I don't know, a portal."

Josh rolled his eyes. "You've been watching too many movies. There has to be a logical way to get there. You need a concrete plan in mind before you decide to go wandering all over a place we aren't familiar with. This isn't Swans Landing. We don't know anyone here and we don't know who we can trust to help us."

I bit my lip. No way could I tell Josh about Callum. He'd freak and then blame me for wandering off on my own. It wasn't like I'd gone out in search of someone to reveal our secret to. How was I supposed to know that some guy would sneak up on me during what was supposed to be a private moment?

"Fine," I said. "You make the plan, since you're the one with the map."

After breakfast—Josh had a peanut butter sandwich and water, gag, while I had three candy bars—we headed down the main street of Pierowall. Now that I wasn't in a rush to get away from everything, I could take some more time to look at the village, which was made up of mostly gray stone buildings and houses. I'd never before understood the definition of *quaint* or why people would describe something in that way, but if there was ever a time to use that word it was now. Pierowall was quaint. The homes were small, squat things with storybook chimneys rising from their roofs. Green fields and pastures rolled out to one side of the village, where cattle grazed, and on the other side, the semicircle bay sparkled and the shadow of Papa Westray emerged as the sun burned off the morning haze. The grass here was brighter than anything I had ever seen, a green so vivid and alive it almost hurt to look at it. Sunlight glittered on the water like it was full of diamonds.

But it wasn't only the village itself that captured my attention, it was the vibrations I felt. They flowed up from the earth under my feet and hung in the salty air. This land was old and alive, and it called out to the finfolk part of me.

The village seemed to have enchanted even Josh. His gaze roamed over our surroundings for a moment, then he said, "It's really nice here. Almost reminds me of home, in a way."

The reminder of Swans Landing sent a sting through me and I crossed my arms, sniffing and tossing my hair over my shoulder, though the wind blew it right back into my face. "It's okay," I contradicted. "Nothing special."

We were used to walking everywhere we went, so we didn't mind going on foot as we searched for any clue that might lead us to the finfolk. We explored the northwestern part of the island, studying the small gray homes and the coastline of Pierowall Bay. We walked as close to the edge of the cliffs as we dared. We stared out at the sea, looking for any unexplained landmasses within the shifting fog. The clouds had a way of rolling in suddenly, obscuring the horizon for a moment, then lifting to reveal clear skies and seas. It was easy to see how an island could become lost within them.

But despite all of that, we found nothing that brought us any closer to the finfolk homeland. I began to doubt it was even near Westray. Maybe we were on the wrong island. Maybe the fact that this island had Mara's last name was a coincidence and not a clue.

"There has to be something here." Josh sifted grains of sand and broken blades of grass through his fingers. We sat in the field near the lighthouse, listening to the wind howling over the cliffs and the caw of birds as they circled through the air around us. We had brought our lunch—peanut butter sandwiches—and created a makeshift picnic.

"Everything has been a dead end." I pulled a piece of the crust off my sandwich and tossed it into the air, watching as four birds dove for it. There was a brief in-air battle, until one of the birds triumphantly snatched the crust away from the others and then flew off to eat it. "I don't think the answer is here."

"It can't be coincidence. It's not just Mara's name. My dad—" He cleared his throat. "Our dad wrote about these islands. He had come here once, the year before he married my mother. He was searching for something and he wrote about coming to northern Orkney."

I ignored the pang that shot through my stomach and focused on my lunch. I didn't know much about my daddy, other than his name, Oliver Canavan. He had been married and his wife about to give birth when he and my mother first became involved.

And then he had died, drowned, in uncertain circumstances.

But I had no stories of him. No one had ever told me who he was, what he liked, what he wanted in his life.

"What was he looking for?" I asked, hugging my knees to my chest.

Josh shook his head. "I'm not sure. A key of some kind. My mom found me reading his papers and she took them away. I think she burned them all."

We sat in silence for a while. The wind whistled around us, and in the distance I could hear the lowing of cows grazing along the rolling grassy hills. The air was thick with salt, as if the land were a part of the sea in a way. It was a good place for finfolk to live. I felt stronger on land here than I had in Swans Landing. The vibrations of the earth were different, more invigorating.

"He was a marine biologist, you know," Josh said after a moment. His face was turned toward the horizon, where hazy fog drifted along the surface of the sea.

I hadn't known this. I had never thought before to ask what it was our father did for a living.

"From reading his papers, I could tell he loved the ocean," Josh went on. "He was drawn to it, probably by the finfolk genes inside him. He wanted to study it and the life within it."

I smirked as I pulled at the grass near my feet. "Too bad none of his college textbooks could tell him about the finfolk. He had to get closer to them in order to study them."

We both fell silent. We knew how this story ended. Oliver Canavan spent time with the finfolk, listening to them sing in the water during the new moon, getting to know them. Getting to know my mama. For which he lost his life.

I had visited his grave once. He was buried in the only cemetery in Swans Landing, right behind the little white church in the center of the island. I had been eleven years old, and my curiosity about the man who had fathered me had gotten to be too much, so I'd walked the short distance from our house to the graveyard.

His headstone had been gray and weathered like the others around it. It didn't stand out in any way, and it had taken me a few minutes to find it as I walked through the graves, reading names of people I didn't know. There were other Canavans in the cemetery since the family had lived in Swans Landing for several generations. Oliver Canavan lay among them, nothing special that made his grave any different.

I had stood in front of it for a long time, hoping to feel something that would let me know this really was my daddy lying in the ground. I didn't know what exactly I had hoped for. Maybe some kind of residual connection to my mama still left in the air around him.

But there had been nothing. He remained, as he had always been, a name of a man who had once existed. He had died before I was born. I didn't know if he had even known my mother was pregnant, or if he would have been happy that he had created me.

I closed my eyes and lifted my face toward the pale sun that barely broke through the gray clouds overhead. The scent of rain hung in the air, though it hadn't yet started to fall.

"It was probably torture," Josh said quietly. "Feeling this urge toward the ocean, but not being able to be a part of it. Not like he wanted to be."

I opened my eyes again and studied Josh's profile. We didn't look much alike. My delicate features were a contrast to Josh's more prominent ones. I had never seen a picture of our father. Whenever I tried to imagine him in my mind, his face was always a blank. Being partially finfolk, our daddy would have been Scottish and most likely some other western European blood was mixed in from his human ancestors as well. Josh had his mama's light brown skin and dark hair and eyes, but his features weren't hers. How much of our daddy was in his face?

"Do you think he wanted to be finfolk?" I asked. "To change forms?"

"He never said so in his papers, not any of the ones I read. But if he had been given the choice, I think he would have chosen a life tied to the water. He already had, as much as a human could."

I laughed harshly. "A half-life, stuck somewhere between human and not. Hiding who we are, always afraid of what might happen if the rest of the world finds out about us." I shook my head. "He should have been thankful he couldn't change."

Josh gave me an annoyed scowl. "I thought you hated humans, and were glad not to be like them."

I looked away, digging my fingernails into my palms. "I don't hate them. I hate how they take their place in this world for granted. They live such easy, simple lives, and yet all they do is complain."

"Not everything is as simple as it looks."

I shrugged. "Maybe, but here's the simple fact: If our daddy hadn't been so caught up in trying to be something he wasn't, maybe he wouldn't have died. This obsession he had with the water is what killed him."

Josh tore up a handful of grass, letting the wind sweep the blades from his open palm. "And if he hadn't been so obsessed, maybe you wouldn't have been born."

I smirked as I clambered to my feet, brushing sand and grass from my jeans. "And that would have made everyone much happier."

Chapter 7

Josh was already up when I rolled myself out of my bunk the next morning. He was eating a peanut butter sandwich, which he had eaten for breakfast, lunch, and dinner the day before.

"Aren't you tired of peanut butter?" I asked.

Josh shrugged. "I eat a lot of peanut butter at home. I'm used to it."

I bit my lip, feeling guilty for how little I knew about Josh's home life. He never talked much about life with his mama. The only thing I knew about Silvia Canavan was that she was prone to panic attacks that would make her act crazy and yell things. Especially when she was around finfolk. I assumed she hadn't always been that way, but for as long as I could remember, she'd been the island lunatic.

I didn't know what to say or if Josh wanted me to say anything, so I decided not to comment and went into the bathroom to change and pull my hair into a messy bun. When I returned to our room, Josh had finished his sandwich and was brushing crumbs off his pants.

He watched as I grabbed my shoes, which were a pair of sandals. "Where are you going?"

"Out," I said. "Running."

"Since when do you run?"

"Since now." I didn't meet Josh's gaze as I buckled the straps around my feet. I wanted to go back to the lighthouse, to see if Callum would be there again. I'd stayed awake most of the night, staring up at the ceiling with an uneasy feeling deep in my stomach. I had been too careless to let Callum hear me, but I couldn't shake the feeling that he knew a lot more than he was saying. I needed to get a better idea of what that might be before I told Josh about him.

"You're running in sandals?" Josh asked.

I sighed. "Sandals are all I have. I'll make do."

Josh stood. "I'll come with you."

"No," I said quickly. "I mean, I want some time alone."

Instantly, Josh's expression darkened. "We shouldn't go off alone. We don't know who or what might be here. This isn't Swans Landing—"

"I know that!" I let out a long breath to calm my irritation. Sometimes Josh treated me like I was a small child. We were only a year apart in age. He wasn't that much more mature than I was. "I want ten minutes to myself. I'm not used to having someone hovering around all the time. Don't you remember what it was like to be alone?"

49

Josh's jaw twitched, his forehead creased into a frown. "Being alone isn't always a good thing." But he sat back down on his bunk and waved a hand. "Go. If you're not back in an hour, I'm coming after you."

I hurried away from the hostel and down the road toward the lighthouse. I knew Josh would be true to his word and I'd have only a short time to find Callum. I needed to know what exactly he knew or thought he knew, and then find a way to keep him quiet.

As I approached the cliff where the lighthouse stood watch over the cold ocean, I spotted a lone figure standing in the grass, his back to me. The bright red hair that blew in the wind was unmistakable.

"So do you really come here every day, or were you hoping to see me again?" I asked as I stepped to his side.

Callum's lips curled into a smile, but he didn't look at me. "Is that a pickup line?"

"You wish." I crossed my arms, shivering in the cool morning. "So you heard me sing yesterday."

He nodded. "Aye, I did. You have a beautiful voice. But then, you should, shouldn't you? It's in your genes."

"You don't know anything about me," I said.

"I know your name is Sailor, and that you are a long way from home."

A cold blast of wind howled over the cliff's edge. Birds swooped around on the currents as they dove back to their perches along the rock wall under our feet.

"Look," I said, "I think you're confused. I'm just a tourist. Whatever it is you think you know, forget about it."

His green eyes twinkled. "You remind me of my sister."

"What?" I asked, startled by the unexpected response.

He turned back to the water. "Her name was Pearl, and she really was one. A gem from the ocean."

He didn't say anything else and instead, turned and starting walking away from the cliff, back in the direction of the village. I followed after him, hurrying through the tall grass.

"Who are you?" I asked him.

"I told you my name," Callum said. "What else do you want to know?"

"Are you—" I couldn't say the word. I couldn't risk revealing myself if he wasn't who I thought he might be. I studied him hard, looking for any sign that he might be something other than an ordinary guy.

"Was there something you wanted from me?" Callum asked, stopping suddenly.

I skidded to a stop on the wet grass, only inches from him. My nose was level with his chin and I could see light freckles scattered across his cheeks.

"N-no," I stammered. "I don't want anything from you."

"Then if you don't mind, I must be going," Callum said. "Unless you plan to follow along and ask me half-questions all day."

He started across the field again and I watched him make his way through the grass. Panic seized my stomach, curling it into tight knots. He knew more than he was saying, I was certain. If he told anyone I'd be in huge trouble. Josh would kill me. The humans might even do it themselves if they found out about us.

"Wait!"

Callum stopped and waited as I ran toward him, already feeling breathless.

"Don't tell anyone about me," I said.

He raised an eyebrow. "What would I tell?"

I glared at him. "You know what I mean."

Several seconds of silence passed between us, with only the sound of the wind and ocean in my ears.

"And if I did tell?" Callum asked. "What would you do?"

"I—I'll—" My brain couldn't think fast enough to come up with a response. I hadn't expected him to challenge my threat. "You'll regret it. So don't."

He laughed, his face breaking into a rosy glow. "Aye, I'm certain I would. Don't worry. Your secret is safe with me."

The wind whipped strands loose from my messy bun as I watched Callum disappear beyond a hill. I let out a frustrated sigh. I was done with mysterious Scottish psychos. I pushed all thoughts of Callum Murchadh out of my mind.

I met Josh on the road to the hostel. It had obviously been longer than an hour, judging from the deep scowl on his face.

"We have a lot of work to do," Josh said. "We need to explore more of the island today."

"I'm tired," I whined.

"You weren't tired a few minutes ago when you decided to go exercise," Josh said. He looked me up and down. "How was your run anyway? You look remarkably well rested for someone who ran for an hour."

"It was fine," I growled, stomping past him.

We left Pierowall and headed along the narrow road away from the village, back in the direction of Rapness Pier where the ferry had dropped us off two days before. Every few steps, Josh would stop to examine random things—a rock, a hill, an abandoned building. He even suspiciously eyed a cow chewing cud near a wooden fence for a while. But we found nothing out of the ordinary. If anything, the vibrations that were so strong closer to the village seemed to fade slightly the farther away we traveled.

"I don't think there's anything here," Josh said a few hours later. We stood near the ruins of an old home, but it was just a home that had once belonged to humans. There was no trace of finfolk anywhere around it.

"There has to be something on this island somewhere," I said, my gaze scanning over the water a few yards from us. "Don't you feel something different about this place?"

"I do," Josh said. "But I don't know where to go from here. If we could find someone we could talk to."

My stomach twisted. I had to tell Josh about Callum. It was the only clue we had.

"There's someone who might know something."

Josh's head whipped toward me. "What?"

I told him about meeting Callum, and what he had said.

Josh ran a hand over his short hair. "Great."

I scowled. "How was I supposed to know some guy

would follow me?"

He shook his head. "What's done is done. But maybe we should go talk to him."

My heart skipped a panicked beat. "Do you think we can trust him?"

"I don't know, but he seems like he knows something. He might be able to point us in the right direction."

Chapter 8

Finding Callum was easier than we thought it would be. Josh had the idea to ask Fiona at the hostel if she knew him, figuring since it was a small village, there was a good chance she would.

"Aye," Fiona said, nodding as she sorted through papers at the front desk. "He lives down the way, over the hill. Wee gray house on your left. You can't miss it."

We followed the main road through Pierowall, looking for the small gray house Fiona had mentioned. The only problem was, most of the houses were small and gray. There wasn't much to differentiate one from another.

Luckily, we were saved from having to knock on every door by the sight of Callum sitting on the front stoop of a home near the end of the row. He sat in a weathered rocking chair, holding a cracked brown mug in his hands. My stomach tightened.

"There he is," I whispered to Josh.

Callum merely nodded a greeting to us as we walked up the cobbled path to his house. He gave me a brief glance before letting his gaze settle on Josh.

"Hello," Callum said. "Callum Murchadh. Welcome."

"Josh Canavan," he answered. "I guess you know my sister, Sailor Mooring."

Callum's eyes twitched slightly and his gaze darted toward me.

"What?" I asked.

Callum shook his head. "This is your first time in Orkney?"

"Yes, it is," Josh answered.

"Here for any reason in particular?"

"Vacationing," Josh said. "We wanted to explore a bit before we headed off to college."

He may have been a know-it-all, but Josh was also a good liar.

Callum nodded. "I've done a bit of traveling myself these last few years."

"Find anything interesting?" I asked.

"Maybe," Callum said, glancing at me again. "How do you like your visit so far?"

"It's nice," Josh answered. "The village is..."

"Quaint," Callum said, smirking over his cup.

Josh's gaze met mine and he sent me a silent warning not to ask any of the questions on the tip of my tongue. I swallowed hard, my tongue scratching against the roof of my mouth.

"Are you from around here?" Josh asked.

"Around," Callum said vaguely. "I've spent my whole life among these islands."

I wanted so much to ask if he knew anything about the finfolk, but I couldn't. It was too dangerous to reveal our secret.

"Care for a cuppa?" Callum asked, gesturing toward his drink.

Josh stuck his hands into the pocket of his hoodie and shook his head. "No, thank you. Actually...we came to ask you a few questions. If you don't mind."

Callum raised one eyebrow.

Josh's gaze darted around the area. There was no one close enough to hear us, but Josh still looked nervous.

"Could we go somewhere private to talk?" he asked at last, turning back to Callum.

Callum scratched his cheek, his eyes locked on us, then nodded as he slowly pushed himself up from his chair. "Come inside."

Inside, the front room was small and dark. The sun barely made it through the thin curtain over the one window to light the room. The furniture was old and mismatched, a few chairs and side tables scattered almost at random throughout the room, as if they'd been added only as an afterthought and without much care.

Josh and I sat down on an old small couch covered with a ragged afghan. Callum eased himself into a chair across from us, still clutching his mug in his hands.

The room was quiet for a long moment, then Josh said, "Can you tell us about your sister?"

I cast an impatient look at him. He had come here to ask Callum about his family?

Callum looked amused. "What about her?"

"You told Sailor that your sister was a 'gem from the ocean.' What exactly do you mean by that?"

The two stared at each other for a long moment, neither speaking or moving. Somewhere within the house, I could hear the tick of a clock, slow and steady.

"She was a beautiful, kind woman," Callum said at last. "Kinder than she should have been in many cases. Patient and accepting."

"Anything else?" Josh asked.

"What else do you think there might be?" Callum responded.

"Something more," Josh said.

Callum's gaze drifted to me and I swallowed hard. "Your sister is something more than what she seems, is she not? What did you say your last name was? Mooring?"

I wasn't sure whether to confirm or deny this, but Josh nodded. "Yes, she has her mother's family's name. I have our father's name. We're half-siblings."

Callum took a slow sip from his cup. His Adam's apple bobbed as he swallowed.

"People say these islands are magic," he said after a moment. "Strange things happen around here. People vanish without a trace. Whole islands appear and disappear within the sea."

I knew if I let this go on, they'd continue this stupid dance around the truth all day, each trying to outsmart the other. This was stupid. Callum had already heard me sing, and he must have known what the song was.

"Tell us what you know," I said, crossing my arms. Now Callum's bright green eyes flicked to me. "I might, if you ask the right questions."

"Are you always this irritating, or are we special?" I let out a frustrated sigh, then said, "What do you know about finfolk?"

Now Callum's smile stretched wide and he had the look of a contented cat about to trap its prey. "Now we can get somewhere." He pointed at me. "You are as finfolk as they come." He looked back at Josh. "And I would assume you are as well, though you don't have a finfolk name."

"I am," Josh admitted. "Through my great-grandmother on my father's side."

"Do you know what her last name was?"

"Moray," Josh answered.

I couldn't hide my surprise at this. I'd known our daddy was finfolk through his grandmother, but I hadn't known which family she came from since I knew so little about him. The Morays were no longer in Swans Landing. The last of them had left when I was young, unable to deal with the harassment finfolk endured back home.

"I knew some Morays once. Good people." Callum set his cup on a table and leaned forward. "Aye, Pearl was more than ordinary. Like you, she was finfolk."

"And so are you," Josh said.

Callum inclined his head once. "I was, at one time."

I blinked, not understanding his words. "You *were?* What does that mean? How could you stop being finfolk?"

"Genetically, I am still finfolk," Callum said. "But I

can no longer take the form. I'm banished, an outsider, and therefore I have no right to claim the heritage. I have been...remade."

"Banished from where?" Josh asked.

My breath got stuck somewhere in my chest when Callum said, "Hether Blether. The vanishing isle."

We were silent for a long time, each staring at the other but afraid to speak.

"So it does exist," Josh said at last.

Callum nodded again. "It exists, though not in the way it once did."

"What do you mean?" I asked, feeling panic rising inside me. I had come all this way and now I was so close. It had to exist.

"What do you hope to find there?" Callum asked, ignoring my question.

I didn't want to tell him about my mama. He didn't have a right to hear the sad tale of poor Sailor Mooring, abandoned as a baby.

"We're looking for answers," Josh said when I didn't respond. I shot him a warning look, but he went on, ignoring me. "We need to find out what happened the night our father died, and we think the one person who can tell us might be in Hether Blether."

I was thankful Josh didn't mention that the person we were looking for was my mother. Callum tilted his head as he examined us.

"What makes you think this person made it to Hether Blether?" he asked. "It is not easy to find, as you already know. If it was, everyone would know where to look for it."

"She's been missing for sixteen years," I said. "She

left to go there, and it's the only clue we have."

"There were once thousands of finfolk around Orkney. But when humans started migrating to this part of Europe, some left in search of other land to claim. The finfolk in Orkney sing for lost souls, but no one answers."

Josh and I exchanged a look.

"We sing," he said. "In Swans Landing—that's the island where we live—all of the finfolk there sing on the first night of the new moon each month."

"I suppose it is a little too far away to hear from here," Callum said. "Has anyone ever answered your call?"

I shook my head. "No. No one ever comes back."

"One person did," Josh said. "Mara."

I rolled my eyes. "I don't think the song had anything to do with bringing Mara back to Swans Landing."

Josh shrugged. "Still, she came back."

I shook my head, disgusted at Josh for finding an excuse to bring up Mara. How far did I have to swim before I could get away from her?

"It is not likely the person you're looking for made it all the way from the States back to Hether Blether," Callum said. "That would be an almost impossible journey."

"We made it this far," Josh pointed out. "We only need to finish the last part of the journey."

"It's the only place we can start looking for her," I added. "So will you take us there or not?"

Callum's green eyes turned darker as he looked at me. Muscles along his cheeks twitched and his Adam's apple bobbed as he swallowed. I squeezed my fists together in my lap as I stared back at him, refusing to break his gaze.

Finally, he said, "No."

All of the air seemed to escape my lungs and my body sunk into the couch. "No?" I repeated, unable to believe I had heard him correctly.

"I left the island five years ago," he said. "I vowed to never return."

I had the urge to throw something at him. How could he sit there, so calm and uncaring, while he possibly held the secret to my finally reaching my mother after all these years?

Josh, apparently sensing my near tantrum, reached over and put his large hand over my small ones in my lap.

"We need your help," Josh said. "If you can't take us there, can you at least tell us where to go?"

"The island vanishes and moves," Callum said. "The fog hides it and not everyone can see it. It is only visible at certain times, for the briefest moment, and still, there is no guarantee you'll reach its shores before it's gone again."

All of my hope slipped away at Callum's words. A vanishing, moving island would be impossible to find.

"We have to try," Josh said. "On our own, if you won't help us."

Callum shook his head. "It will be a wasted effort. But if you insist, there is a way to increase your odds of finding it."

"How?" Josh leaned forward, practically on the edge of his seat.

"There is a key," Callum said. "Nothing very significant about it, except that the person who holds it at the right moment on the right night in the right sea might find their way to Hether Blether."

"Then give us the key and we'll go on our own!" I exclaimed, the words bursting from my mouth.

Callum shrugged. "I don't have it."

I leaped from my seat, lunging at Callum, my hands outstretched. I didn't know what I might have done if I'd reached him, maybe shook him hard until he agreed to take us to the finfolk or else pummeled him with my fists until I felt better. But Josh saved him from whatever fate might have awaited him by grabbing my waist and pulling me backward. We tumbled onto the couch, a tangle of arms and legs, and Josh held me tight against him.

"Sailor," he growled in my ear. "Calm down."

"He can help us!" I said, struggling to get away. "He knows where it is, but he's too stubborn to help. He's like all the stories say about finfolk, as mean as the old legends."

"If he doesn't want to help, he doesn't have to," Josh said.

I stopped struggling, slumping against Josh. He didn't let go, apparently not trusting that all the fight had gone out of me. "It doesn't matter anyway," I said. "You're probably too much of a bastard to be susceptible to pain."

Callum laughed, which caused Josh to laugh too. Josh finally let me go and pushed me off of him. He stood and then extended a hand to Callum.

"Thank you for your time," he said. "If you happen

to think of anything that might be helpful to us, please let us know."

Josh gestured for me to follow as he walked toward the door. I shot a dark scowl at Callum, feeling anger surge through me again when he smiled back. It took every ounce of willpower inside me not to throw one of his dusty old lamps at his head on my way out.

Once we were outside, Josh paused and let out a long sigh. I stopped next to him and surveyed the village laid out along the narrow road before us.

"What do we do now?" I asked.

Josh shook his head. "I wish I knew."

Chapter 9

Fiona was in the front room folding towels when we returned to the hostel. She greeted us with, "I trust you found Callum?"

"We did, thank you," Josh said.

"Not that it helped," I muttered.

"Well, if you're in the mood for exploring more of the island today, there is a heritage museum nearby," she said. "Worth looking into if you want to know more about Westray."

"Thanks," Josh said. "We'll take a look later."

He stomped down the hall to our room, his shoulders slumped under his thick hoodie. I followed him into the room and sat down in the chair in the corner, watching as he reached for his bag and pulled out a notepad he must have bought at the general store yesterday.

He sat down on the bed, propped the notepad on one

knee and began writing.

"What are you doing?" I asked.

"Writing a letter." He didn't look up.

I made a face. "There's this thing called email and text messages now."

"Still can't get a signal on my phone," Josh said.

I stared out the window for a moment. The people of Pierowall never seemed to be in a hurry. They always moved lazily down the street, as if they had no reason to rush things. No one seemed to feel the need to escape.

The sound of Josh's pen scratching across the paper irritated me.

"Who are you writing to?" I asked.

Josh scowled before bending back over his letter. "None of your business."

I knew that could only mean he was writing to Mara. Probably some sappy, lovesick letter about how much he missed her and how he dreamed about her every night.

"You shouldn't waste your time on her," I said.

Josh ignored me and continued writing.

"She's probably not even missing you," I went on. "You're four thousand miles away, on the other side of the ocean, and she's in Swans Landing. With Dylan."

I hated to think about the idea of Dylan and Mara taking comfort in each other, but I knew it was the only logical conclusion to this messed up tangle of hormones. Dylan didn't want me. He had never, despite the fact that we'd been friends our entire lives, looked at me the way he'd looked at Mara as soon as she stepped foot on the island.

If Josh thought Dylan wouldn't take advantage of his not being around right now, he was stupid and naive. The island had a way of making people lonely, lonelier than they'd ever felt before. And the longer Josh was gone, the closer Mara would move to Dylan in search of company.

Josh's nostrils flared as he stared back at me. "Don't talk to me about Dylan Waverly," he growled.

I shrugged. "I'm only trying to make you see reality. She's been in his bed once. How long do you think it will be before she's there again?"

Before I had time to react, Josh leaped from the bed and across the room, suddenly hovering over me. His face was red, his eyes dark and narrowed. I'd made him angry before, even irritated him as much as possible for the fun of it, but I'd never seen him look at me the way he did now.

"If you know what's good for you, Sailor Mooring, you'll shut your mouth about things you have no business being involved in," he said in a low, raspy voice.

I'd read things on finfolk before, looking up myths and beliefs humans had about them and laughing at how inaccurate some of them were. But as I looked up at Josh's stony face, something from one of those books flashed across my mind: *Finfolk are extremely territorial.*

Right at that moment, Josh was more finfolk than he realized.

I held up my hands. "No need to go all psycho on me."

Josh stepped back, the fury fading from his face,

though his forehead was still crinkled into a scowl. "Don't mention anything else about Dylan in front of me," he growled.

Who would have known Josh would be the jealous type? I filed this information away for future use should the need arise.

"Whatever." I stood and headed for the door.

"Where are you going?" he asked.

"Out," I said.

I was thankful Fiona was no longer in the front lobby as I made my way out of the hostel. I wasn't in the mood to talk to anyone, and she looked like someone who enjoyed talking. I sidestepped an elderly couple walking arm-in-arm down the street, then took a look around, trying to decide where to go.

Something called me toward the lighthouse, but I didn't want to risk Callum Murchadh seeing me pass. I was not in the mood for dealing with him again so soon. So instead, I turned the other way and found myself facing the sign for the Pierowall Heritage Museum.

The building was small and quiet. Soft music played over the sound system and the only other people perusing the displays were a family with two young kids who looked bored and ready to go, tugging at their parents' hands. The parents remained bent over one display, reading the information card attached to it.

"Mum, let's go," the little girl said, tugging at her mother's arm.

"All right, love," her mom said, finally stepping away from the display. "We're going."

I turned my back to the mother-daughter pairing and

started at the opposite end of the room. The displays were all about the history of Westray and Pierowall, from the ancient people who first lived there to the modern day. I studied the artifacts and other pieces that made up the heritage of the island, moving through the displays as my eyes quickly scanned over the words on the cards.

When I reached the end—the family had finally left —I stopped and looked back across the room. That was it? There were several pieces in the collection, but no mention of finfolk anywhere.

A middle aged man approached me, smiling wide. "I trust you've enjoyed your visit to our heritage museum," he said. "I would be happy to help with any questions you may have, or fill in additional information on the pieces."

He was short, a couple inches shorter than I was, and he was round and rosy-cheeked, with graying hair just above his ears. I wasn't sure that I wanted to reveal what I was most interested in to this man.

"Is there any information on other parts of Westray?" I asked. "Like, myths and legends?"

The man scratched at the light stubble along his chin. "Like fairy legends?"

I cringed. I hated when finfolk were compared to fairies. "Yes," I forced myself to say. "Do you have information on those?"

"You'll want the Fae Museum for that. It's down the road, to the right. A little building next to McIntyre's Pub. Look for the fairy on the door."

I nodded and then left the heritage museum. It was probably a waste going to something called a "Fae

Museum." Likely the only thing I'd find would be tales about little creatures that granted wishes or stole babies or whatever it was fairies supposedly did in this part of the world.

Without looking for it, I probably would have passed the Fae Museum by without a second glance. The building looked like all the other gray stone buildings around it, and it was small and tucked almost behind the pub.

A cracked cobblestone path led the way to the door with a copper fairy on it and I turned the knob slowly, cringing when the door creaked, the sound echoing throughout the room. It was small and dark, but there was a cozy feeling to the place and light, tinkling music played from a stereo in one corner. The walls were covered with paintings of fairies and other mythical creatures. A few fairy "artifacts" had been scattered throughout the room on tables, mixed among fairy figurines.

A woman emerged from a hallway, smiling wide when she saw me.

"Welcome!" she boomed, throwing her arms wide as she came at me. Before I could react, I found myself enveloped in a hug. "A seeker of the fae, are you? Aye, you've come to the right place. Come, look around. If you have any questions, I'll be certain to answer them. I'm the resident expert on the fae around here." She grinned, her face crinkling into shiny cheeks and bright white teeth.

"Um," I said, extricating myself from her embrace. "Thanks. I was wondering about ancient legends."

She grabbed my hand and pulled me toward one of

the displays, pointing out what looked like pieces of rocks. "There are many legends here in Orkney," she told me. "These are pieces of a walking stone. At night, they've been seen walking down the water to take a drink." She moved to the next table, which featured small animal bones. "Fairy bones," she whispered. "A very rare find."

This was definitely a waste of time. "Uh, nice," I said. "Actually, I should get back. My brother is waiting for me."

Her smile faded for a moment, but then she grinned again and gestured toward another display. "Perhaps I can interest you in something else? We have many displays."

I shook my head. "Really, I should go—"

"Are selkies more your interest? Or perhaps finfolk —"

I paused, turning back to look at her as an icy chill raced down my spine. "You have finfolk artifacts here?" I asked.

She grinned and then crooked her finger, gesturing for me to follow her to the other side of the room. She led me to a table in a corner, where only a few pieces were kept under a glass box. One looked like silver fish scales collected inside a plastic bag. Next to it sat a string of seashells tied into a necklace and a few drawings of finfolk creatures either leaping from the water or else crawling on the sand, still with fishtails, with a twisted piece of metal holding the paper in place in one corner.

"The finfolk were once seen often in Orkney," the woman told me. "They used to travel back and forth between their islands and ours. They had many, you know, but the two we know the most about are Hildaland and Hether Blether. Hildaland was taken by a human who tricked them, and now the island lies visible to human eyes south of Rousay. But Hether Blether remains hidden, vanishing within the fog and relocating itself whenever anyone tries to find it."

I looked over the pieces in the display case, but nothing looked authentic to me. "What are those?" I asked, pointing at the fish scales.

"Scales taken from a finfolk," she said, her eyes wide.

They looked more like scales taken from a sea bass to me, but I didn't say this aloud.

"These drawings are from witnesses who have seen finfolk over the years," she went on. "They don't come to our island like they used to. Most of the drawings are very old. That is why we protect them in the glass."

I suppressed a sigh. What had I expected to find in a tiny fairy museum, anyway? It was a dead end run by a woman who didn't seem to have all of her marbles in place.

"I really should go," I said. "Thanks for the tour."

She kept her smile, but I could see the disappointment in her eyes. "Aye okay. Do come back whenever you'd like. And bring your brother. I'm certain he'd love to see our collection."

Somehow, I couldn't imagine Josh pouring over the fairy "artifacts." But I nodded and said, "Sure." Then I escaped into the sunshine, blinking at its sudden brightness.

Well, it was official. Every path in Pierowall had

come to a dead end and I wasn't any closer to finding the way to my mother than I had been before.

Chapter 10

I needed chocolate, preferably the kind full of fat and sugar.

After another long day of pointless searching—this time we'd roamed around hills and farmlands toward the middle of the island—I stepped into the shop across from the hostel, entering into a world of closely packed shelves and soft music. Thunder rumbled outside as the door closed behind me.

The store was empty. My skin prickled at the coldness inside the shop, and I paused, looking around for a moment.

"May I help you?" a voice asked, followed by the appearance of a familiar face coming around one of the aisles.

Callum stopped when he saw me. "Oh," he said.

I couldn't tell if that "oh" was good or bad.

He wore a green apron over his clothes and he bent

to pick up a box of canned beans, which he carried past me to the next aisle.

"You work here?" I asked as I followed him.

"Five days a week," he answered.

"But you're—" I paused, searching for the right word.

Callum's eyebrows knit together. "Disabled?" he asked.

I had forgotten about his prosthetic leg. I couldn't even tell a difference through his jeans.

I shook my head. "That wasn't what I was going to say."

"Aye?" Callum set the box on the floor and began setting cans on a shelf. "What then?"

I glanced around, making sure no one was nearby, and then lowered my voice. "Finfolk."

Callum squatted next to the box. "Finfolk don't have jobs where you're from?"

Heat flooded up my neck. Why was it he could never make a conversation easy?

"Of course they do," I said. "I didn't think...I mean, you live *here* and—"

"And I still require money in order to live among the humans," Callum finished. He turned away from me, smirking as he continued to stock the shelf.

I sighed, feeling a bit frustrated. I wanted to get what I came for and then leave. "Do you have chocolate?" I asked. "Snickers. M&Ms. Butterfinger. Even an Almond Joy will work, and I hate almonds."

"Hates almonds," Callum said, nodding. "I'll file that away for future reference." He jerked his head toward the right. "Two aisles over. You should find what you want there."

I followed his directions and found a selection of various chocolates and candies. It was much smaller than I was hoping for, but it would do. I grabbed several bars of various kinds.

When I made my way to the counter, Callum was already there, waiting for me. Outside, a crack of thunder sounded, followed by a hard, pelting rain on the roof.

"Most finfolk I know aren't so keen on chocolate," Callum commented as he rang up my purchases.

I raised my eyebrows. "And how many finfolk do you know?"

"Many," he said. "But not as many as there should be."

He was quiet as he punched in some keys on the old register. He looked so serious about everything he did, his brow furrowed as he focused on ringing me up. A wave of irritation flooded through me.

"You know, if you'd tell us where to find these finfolk, Josh and I will go on our own," I said. "We don't need you, you don't have to go with us or anything."

Callum snorted. "Your naivety is exactly what would get you killed if you attempted to find them."

I leaned on the counter, my fists clenched. "We need to get to Hether Blether. We've been looking for clues, trying to ask people without bringing up suspicion—"

Callum looked up sharply, anger in his eyes. "You shouldn't be asking anyone about that. You don't know who you can trust."

I laughed. "Like I should trust you? You are the only hope we have and you've done *nothing* to help. You walk around pretending to be human, selling their groceries. You turned your back on who you really are. That's why you were banished, isn't it?"

Callum's eyes narrowed, the color turning a dark green. "Go back to the States, for your own sake and for everyone else's."

"If it'll get me far away from you, gladly." I spun on my heel and stomped across the store. The door flew open as I pushed at it, swinging back to smack the wall of the shop before shutting again.

The heavy, pouring rain that had begun while I was in the store soaked me within seconds. My hair stuck to my face and I paused to push it out of my eyes.

The door opened behind me and uneven footsteps crunched across the gravel parking lot. I turned to find Callum walking toward me, his head ducked slightly. The rain soaked him as quickly as it had me, and his red hair became plastered to his head. The white T-shirt under his apron was thin and I could see the outline of muscled arms and shoulders through the wet cloth.

Water trickled down his face, dripping from his nose and chin as he drew closer to me. I could imagine him emerging from the ocean, halfway between his finfolk and human forms. I wondered what color his scales were, and what he looked like swimming through the water.

My breath caught in my throat as he gazed down at me through the sheets of rain.

He thrust a paper bag at me and I took it, my hands

clasping around the soggy paper.

"You forgot your chocolate," he said. He studied me for a long moment, almost seeming to look through me. Then he turned and walked back into the shop.

* * *

Josh bent over the strings of his borrowed guitar, smiling as he played a few notes. One of the older men with him said something and everyone laughed, the fading sunset illuminating Josh's smile.

I sat on a stone in front of a shop, closed up even though the sun set so late this far north that "night" was still an hour away. Back home, Josh played his guitar in front of Moody's Variety Store, gathered around a roaring fire in an old burn barrel on cold nights. I could tell he missed it from the way his smile stretched across his face while he learned the folk songs the others played.

Anyone who glanced at them would think Josh had played with them all his life. He was so comfortable pretending to be human. He could easily find a place where he fit in among them.

Grandma had taught me to play the fiddle as soon as I was big enough to hold the instrument under my chin. Josh didn't know this. I didn't reveal it to many people.

"Your mama could play beautifully," Grandma once told me. "The fiddle sang in her hands, like it was a part of her."

My fingers twitched, itching to dance over the strings. It had been so long since I'd played that the calluses had worn off my fingers. I clenched my hands into fists and buried them in my lap.

"You should join them," said a voice behind me.

I didn't look up, but I recognized the lilting brogue. "I don't play," I said.

"Liar." Callum eased himself onto another stone near mine, stretching his legs out in front of him. "I see the way you look at them. Let's see if I can guess what you play." He tapped his chin as he grinned. "The bagpipes? You have enough hot air for it."

I shot him a glare before turning my back to him.

"No," he said, "I imagine you to be something with a bit more life to it. Something wee and feisty. Like...the fiddle."

I stiffened, but I didn't acknowledge his guess.

"Looks like your brother fits right in."

"Only because he's good at being something he's not," I said.

"Maybe he isn't pretending. Maybe that is exactly who he is."

I sneered. "He can walk around on land and pretend to be human all he wants. But if they knew who he really was, they'd never accept him."

"You think so?" Callum asked.

"Finfolk don't belong in the human world," I said. "Once we get to Hether Blether, he'll realize that."

Callum's face was half-hidden in shadows, but I could make out the grim line of his mouth. "You might want to wait until you reach Hether Blether before deciding that. Things might not be as you imagine."

I laughed. "They can't possibly be any worse than Swans Landing. You don't know what I've been through, what humans have put me through."

"And you don't know what finfolk have put me through," he said solemnly.

We stared at each other for a long moment, until the band began to play again and their music drifted toward us. The rain earlier in the day had lifted to reveal slightly cloudy skies. People passed by, strolling leisurely as they enjoyed the evening. The wind was chilly, but it felt refreshing in my lungs.

"What are you doing here?" I asked.

Callum shrugged. "I had nothing else to do."

"So you thought you'd come harass me."

He laughed. "Don't think so highly of yourself. I often come to listen to the music. They know a lot of old songs, ones that have been passed down through the generations." When I didn't say anything, he added, "Ones that aren't entirely human in origin."

I understood what he meant. The musicians had played a song earlier that had almost sounded like the music of breaking waves in the ocean. The humans might not know what the song was, believing it to be an old folk song, but any finfolk knew where it had really come from.

"Do you miss your home?" I asked.

"Do you miss yours?"

I thought about home, which made me think about Dylan. My chest ached as I pictured him. He had been my best friend for as long as I could remember. Everything I knew about Swans Landing was wrapped up in Dylan Waverly.

But I didn't want to tell Callum about Dylan. I didn't want to try to explain what he was to me, or what he might have been if things had turned out differently.

"I miss my grandma," I said. "I worry about whether she's okay."

"What about the rest of your family?"

I stiffened. "I don't want to talk about my family."

Callum nodded to where Josh was listening to an old man talk, his eyes wide with interest. "What about your brother?"

"What about him?"

"If you find Hether Blether, are you prepared for the fact that you'll be taking him into danger?" Callum asked.

A chill swept its way up my spine. "What is so bad about Hether Blether?"

Callum sighed. "More than you know."

I remembered the way he'd looked in the rain, his pale skin wet and shining, his hair darkened by the water. I wondered again what he looked like in his finfolk form.

He turned to me, looking into my eyes. There was something there, something I couldn't figure out. I opened my mouth, licking my dry lips.

"What happened to your leg?"

Callum's body visibly stiffened. He turned toward the musicians and didn't answer me.

I could take a hint, especially one as big as what he sent me way. "Then tell me why you're banished from Hether Blether," I said.

Callum shook his head. "It's a long story."

"I have time." Thin wisps of clouds hung in the purple sky. Song night was approaching quickly.

Already, I could feel the pull of the water calling out to me. "Since you're not helping me get where I need to be."

"It is not a nice story," he said. "It will make you think badly of finfolk, maybe even of me as well."

I suppressed a shiver as the wind blew over me, lifting the ends of my hair. "Why? Did you kill someone?"

I had meant it as a joke, expecting him to laugh and roll his eyes. But his face only tightened even further into a grimace.

"Why do you want to find the finfolk so badly?" he asked.

I turned away from him, letting out a sigh. "We told you," I said. "We need to find someone."

"Is this someone really that important?" he asked.

My eyes stung suddenly with tears and I let the wind whip them away before they could trickle down my cheeks. "Yes, she is."

"There is a good chance she never made it to Hether Blether."

I gritted my teeth until my jaw ached. "But there's also a chance that she did. I have to believe that until I find out otherwise."

"What if she's not? What if you came all this way and you somehow get to Hether Blether, and then this person you're looking for is not there?"

It was the exact question I didn't like to think about. I had to trust that my mother had come this way. Maybe she had even once sat in the same spot where I now sat, looking out at the bay and trying to find the way home. I could see her clearly in my head, the young woman that appeared whenever I sang. She had to still exist somewhere, waiting for me to find her.

There wasn't a possibility that she wouldn't be there at the end of this journey. It was the only thing that kept me going.

"If she's not there," I said in a choked voice, "then I'll keep searching. For as long as it takes, wherever I have to go. I'm not going home until I find her, so save your breath. You won't convince me not to keep looking." I shuffled my feet along the grass and rocks. "Haven't you ever had someone that was so important to you, you'd do anything for them?"

Callum turned his face away from me. "Who is she?" he asked, his voice so low I almost couldn't hear him over the sound of the music.

I didn't want to trust him. He hadn't given me any reason to let him have this secret. Except he was finfolk, probably the only pure finfolk I'd ever met, and he hadn't told anyone else about Josh and me.

"She's my mother," I said at last. "She left when I was a few months old, after my daddy died."

Callum shifted closer, his arm brushing mine. "How did your father die?"

Josh played on, oblivious to our conversation. I studied his features, looking again for a face there that I had never seen.

"He drowned."

I could feel Callum's surprise even though I didn't look at him. "Finfolk can't drown," he said.

"My daddy wasn't finfolk. Not fully. His grandma had been finfolk, so he had some of the heritage, but he couldn't change form. He was unlucky enough to fall in love with my mama and he died trying to be with her."

"So you're a half-breed," he said.

My lip curled at the words, the insult some people back in Swans Landing liked to spit at me.

"Don't call me that," I growled through clenched teeth.

"I'm sorry," Callum said. "But you're not fully finfolk. In Hether Blether, that fact matters. If you make it there, you can't let anyone know you're part human. Don't tell them Josh's last name, don't mention your father drowning."

His expression was grim. His mouth was set in a tight, straight line and his eyes had turned a darker green.

"Why?" I asked.

"How many stories about finfolk have you heard where you come from?" he asked. "Do you know what they used to do to humans?"

I shrugged. "I read in a book once that finfolk supposedly abducted humans and married them."

Callum grimaced. "The myths get warped over the years. Yes, finfolk abducted humans. But trust me, Hether Blether is not the place to be human. Be as finfolk as you possibly can. Your last name will help. Mooring is a true finfolk name, and it will offer some protection."

In the traditional sense, Mooring should never have been my name. If my parents had been married or if my mama had followed human traditions, I should have been named Sailor Canavan, like Josh. Maybe because of the circumstances of my birth, my mama had chosen to give me her name instead. But the name Mooring came from Grandma Gale. My granddaddy was human, but he and Grandma had never married, and so she gave my mama her own name.

Twice, I should have had a human name, and yet the name I had was the one thing my family had blessed me with. Maybe the one thing that would help me in Hether Blether, if Callum was right.

But I still had no way of even getting there.

"Why would I need protection," I began slowly, "if you won't help me?"

My mouth went dry as I waited for his response. He was the only hope I had, the only chance of possibly finding my mother.

"I'll help you," he said at last. "I'll take you as far as I can."

I wondered if this was all a joke, if he was toying with me for fun. How much did I really know about this guy? How much could I trust him?

"I thought you didn't have the key," I said.

His mouth twitched. "I don't. But I know where it is."

Chapter 11

My shoes crunched on rocks as I came to a sudden stop at the end of the path.

"I've already been here," I said. The building looked as tiny and forgettable as it had two days ago when I'd visited. Annoyance flashed through me. This was a waste of time, I'd already decided that on my first visit, and I wasn't eager to see it again.

"Follow me," Callum said. He had arrived at the hostel early that morning as the sun broke through the misty fog that hung over the village. I hadn't told Josh where we were going, in case Callum didn't really have the key. I didn't want to get anyone else's hopes up.

It took a moment for my eyes to adjust to the darkness inside the museum. The woman from my earlier visit fussed over Callum, squeezing him in a tight hug as if she hadn't seen him in years.

"Moira," Callum said as she released him, "this is my friend, Sailor."

I didn't have time to consider Callum calling me his friend because the woman turned toward me and her mouth broke into a wide, crooked grin, her eyes flashing in the bit of sunlight that streamed through the open door behind me.

"I knew you'd be back," she said, pointing a finger at me. "You have questions, I can see it in your eyes. I knew you wouldn't be able to stay away."

I ignored Moira's comments and crossed my arms, scowling back at Callum. "So where is it?" I asked.

"Moira," he said, turning to her again, "I need to take back the key I gave you."

Her smile vanished suddenly. "That is one of the best pieces I have in the collection," she protested.

"I have something I can trade for it." He held up a bag in one hand, which he had been carrying but wouldn't tell me what was in it.

Moira took the bag and walked over to an empty table, carefully emptying the contents onto the surface. It was nothing of much interest: a dried starfish, a few shells, and a pointed rock.

"They came from Hether Blether," Callum told her. "The starfish adorned the king's palace. The shells are from a finfolk child's game, and the spear point is from a finfolk guard's weapon."

Moira poured over the items with interest,

captivated by the sight of them. To me, they looked like ordinary objects that Callum could have picked up anywhere. He'd probably found them while walking along the bay of Pierowall. There was absolutely no reason to believe any of these things had actually touched finfolk hands, other than his own.

But Moira seemed satisfied. She nodded and she straightened up. "Aye okay, I'll take the trade," she said. "But only because it's for you. I wouldn't give it up for anyone else."

The little woman led us across the room to the corner where the finfolk display was kept. She carefully lifted the glass box from over the table. I stepped forward, trying to figure out which item was this mysterious key Callum wanted so badly.

Moira's fingers wrapped around the twisted piece of metal that held the drawings in place. She held it in her palm as if it were fragile and offered it to Callum.

"Thank you," Callum told her softly as he took the metal from her.

Moira gazed wistfully at his closed fist. "If you decide you have no use for it, you will consider bringing it back to me?" she asked, a hopeful note in her voice. "I couldn't bear the thought of it ending up somewhere else, in a place where it wouldn't be revered."

Callum squeezed her hand. "I promise, you'll be the first to have it should I no longer need it."

Moira gave a sad smile, but she nodded. Callum said good-bye to her and then we left the little museum, emerging back into the hazy morning.

"That's the key?" I asked, when we were alone.

Callum opened his hand and showed me the piece of metal. It was old and thin, only a narrow, rusty piece of iron. There were no special markings on it. It didn't even look like any key I'd ever seen.

"This was forged in Finfolkaheem," Callum told me. "That was the capitol of the finfolk homeland, a city far below the ocean's surface. It is lost to us now, as are many of the vanishing islands. This key will help guide us to any of the islands we wish to find, though Hether Blether is the only one I know of still in existence."

"How exactly does it work?" I asked.

"We only need to have it with us when we go into the water. The key can feel the pull of the islands and will lead us to the closest one."

I wasn't sure I believed any of this, but at the moment I didn't have another option. "So let's go," I said. "We can get Josh and then search for this island."

Callum shook his head. "It doesn't work that easily."

I tilted my head back and sighed. "Of course not. What now? Some ancient riddle or curse we have to break? Do we need to sacrifice a crab?"

"You watch too much telly," he said. "No, I only meant we can't go because it's not the right time. There is a reason they're called vanishing islands. They only appear during certain times of the month. We have to wait until Monday."

"Why?" I asked.

He smirked. "Do you not know? Can't you feel it?"

Of course. The new moon was two days away. I could feel it inside me, that pull toward the water that was already beginning. On the first night of every new moon, the finfolk back home would go to the water, gathering in the darkness to sing. It was an urge none of us could resist, even during the height of the summer tourist season, when it became dangerous to risk being seen.

"Song Night," I said. "The song calls us home."

"We have to wait until then to try it," Callum said. "And we'll need a boat."

"We're finfolk," I said. "Can't we swim there?"

"*You're* finfolk," Callum corrected me, his voice hardening. "But I told you, I gave up my heritage. I need a boat. I'll take you as far as I can, then you're on your own."

Chapter 12

As Monday night descended on Pierowall, the sky stayed black, unlit by the new moon. Callum met us at the beach along the bay. We had our bags strapped to our backs, all of the few belongings we had packed inside. If all went according to plan, Josh and I would not be returning to Pierowall with Callum that night.

The village of Pierowall sat along a semi-circle bay, which opened out into the cold Atlantic. It was late enough that most of the homes behind us were dark. The lack of a moon in the sky made the night even darker.

A small motorboat sat on the shore, one end bobbing in the gentle waves that washed onto the beach.

"Are you sure we can all fit in that?" I asked, eying

the boat. Josh wasn't exactly a small guy, and though Callum was thin, he was tall. I wasn't sure that even I could fit into the boat comfortably.

"We'll fit," Callum assured me. "Unless you've changed your mind about going to Hether Blether."

I set my jaw and then climbed into the boat, claiming the seat at the front of the bow.

"You'll need to push us off," Callum told Josh. "I can't because..." He gestured toward his prosthetic leg.

Josh nodded and Callum climbed into the boat, settling down in the middle seat. He moved expertly, as if he had done this many times before.

"Where'd you get the boat?" I asked.

"Think I stole it?" Callum challenged.

"I wouldn't put it past you." I wasn't sure how much I should trust him. The way he'd peddled "finfolk artifacts" at the Fae Museum in exchange for the key unnerved me, if in fact they were real. The spearhead from a finfolk guard's weapon sounded like something a person didn't find lying around somewhere. It left me with a sickened feeling in my stomach, and I couldn't help imagining all the ways Callum might have come into possession of things he could barter so easily and without any hesitation.

The other option was that none of the things he had bartered were actually what he claimed they were. And that would mean he had taken advantage of a woman who didn't seem to be all there in her mind.

"I borrowed the boat," Callum told me.

"Borrowed is a vague term." I clutched the sides of

the boat as it rocked when Josh pushed it into the water. "Does the person know you borrowed it?"

"Aye," Callum answered, his tone dry. "I'm not a thief."

I nodded to the twisted metal tucked into his belt. "Then tell me how you got that key."

Callum grinned and winked, but he didn't answer my question.

Josh leaped into the boat, splashing cold water around us. He had to be quick to avoid changing form. Finfolk could delay the change for a few minutes when needed, but eventually it would come if they remained immersed in salt water.

The engine rumbled to life, sputtering and coughing, and then Callum steered the boat into a turn away from the village. My teeth chattered as the cold breeze hit us full force once we were out on the water. New moon was the best time for this journey. It was so dark there were no other boats out for late night fishing, and if anyone looked out the windows of the homes near the shore, they wouldn't be able to make out the little rowboat on the surface of the black water.

We left the bay and ventured into the water between Westray and Papa Westray. Then we turned east into the black night.

The water became rougher the farther we went from land. Our little boat bobbed and pitched on top of the waves, sea spray bursting around us in white foam. If we had been human, the adventure in the little boat might have been dangerous. We could have tipped at any moment among the bouncing waves. But being finfolk allowed us the luxury of not having to worry about drowning out in the cold Atlantic.

I perched on the front of the boat, leaning as far over the edge as I could without losing my balance. My eyes scanned the dark night around us, but I couldn't see anything except blackness in every direction. There were no signs of an island anywhere.

"So how do you know we're going in the right direction?" I yelled to Callum over the motor.

He cut the engine, letting the boat drift on the water. He held the twisted metal clasped tightly between his hands. His eyes were closed, his face contorted in a pained expression.

After a moment, he opened his eyes. "We're going in the right direction," he said. "The key will lead us."

I looked beyond him to Josh, trying to pass a silent message to him. I couldn't feel anything that told me we were going the right way. I had expected *something*. This was Song Night. The whole purpose of the song was to call us home, so I thought I should hear or feel something.

Josh didn't look worried as he studied the darkness around us. He seemed to trust Callum to lead the way, as if there was no reason not to.

Callum started the engine again and we sped farther away from Westray and into the black night. The boat pitched again and I grasped the edge tight. I leaned over the side, peering down into the water. It was too dark to even see my reflection. Water sprayed up into my face, leaving a salty taste on my lips. It had been too long since I'd been in the water. After the two month swim, I didn't think I'd care to be immersed again, but now I felt the craving building inside me. My body urged me to dive deep. It was Song Night. It was what I was supposed to do, what I had always done my entire life.

I reached a hand down, plunging my fingers into the icy liquid. The ocean's vibrations flowed up my arm, making the hair along my skin stand on end. Dizziness and nausea washed over me. It wasn't right to fight against my natural urge, not on this night. This night was meant for the water.

Golden sparks flashed at the corners of my vision before I heard it. A soft song flowed up from the water around me. The song of the Atlantic, the one that had been ingrained into me from birth.

I shouldn't have been able to hear it. The motor still sputtered and roared behind me, yet the song was clear in my ears over the noise.

A laugh from the water bubbled up next to me. I leaned closer to the surface, perched precariously over the edge of the boat. It was all I could do to keep from plunging my face in. I searched the shadows, my fingers digging into the wood.

Then I saw her. The face appeared in the water in front of me, below the surface. She smiled up at me, looking as young and vibrant as she did in the photos in Grandma's album back home. She looked alive and happy and she lifted a hand toward me.

"Mama!" I called, reaching for her.

"Sailor!" someone behind me shouted. But the shout sounded far away and muffled. It didn't sound real. My mother, swimming in the water below me, *that* was real. She was calling me home, leading me to her.

I stood in the rocking boat, pausing only long enough to kick off the sandals I wore, and then I dove, arcing through the night air, toward the roiling water below.

Chapter 13

The water enveloped me, the current sucking me away
from the boat and the two faces that peered over the
side. One more rolling wave and darkness obscured
my vision as I slipped deeper under the surface. The
change overtook me when I opened my mouth and let
water rush in. My bones cracked and popped as they
reformed themselves. I had worn a dress specifically
so I wouldn't have to worry about clothing in the
water, but I had to quickly slip out of my underwear,
letting it float away in the current. The skin between
my toes stretched like rubber bands as my feet fused
and spread into a wide tail fin. Red and silver scales
replaced the bronzed skin from my waist all the way
down to my feet.

I was the other me once again. Changing form

always made me feel giddy, as if I was only truly myself once I was in the water and could be finfolk.

The song was stronger now, wrapped all around me. I couldn't see my mother anywhere and for a moment, it was just me, floating within the black sea.

A splash and an explosion of bubbles signaled someone else's arrival, but the water was too black to see the face of the person next to me.

Then I saw her again, my mother swimming farther below us. I shouldn't have been able to see her that far away in the dark water, but she created her own light, glowing somehow. A part of me knew it wasn't real, that it was the effects of the song on my mind. The finfolk song made humans see what they wanted most. It was why people had believed for centuries that mermaid-like creatures could lure humans to their deaths through song. The humans became so entranced in what they saw they would do anything to get to it.

I wasn't fully finfolk, so the song affected me too.

Even though I knew this, I also knew that the visions the song had given me before now had never looked as vibrant or as real as my mama looked right then. She was solid, not hazy like I'd always seen her. I could reach out and touch her, certain I'd feel actual skin if I did.

I couldn't let her get away. Not when she'd never been this real before.

I dove deeper, following the glowing light of my mother as she darted through the water. I could almost swear I heard her laugh mixed into the song around me. She was quick and I had to swim hard to keep up with her. The current pushed me back, but I fought to reach her. She dove farther into the black depths of the ocean and my mind swirled with dizziness as exhaustion overtook me.

My mama was now a barely visible glow in the darkness far below me. I reached toward her, calling out, but the only thing that left my mouth was a stream of bubbles.

A hand grasped my arms under the armpits, snatching me up. I didn't have the energy to fight, so I let myself be pulled toward the surface.

Callum bobbed in the water next to me, his hair wet and stuck to his forehead. His shirt was soaked through and plastered to his shoulders.

"What the hell is wrong with you?" he asked.

I opened my mouth, but his outburst had taken me by surprise and I couldn't find a response. He didn't wait, but dove under the surface again. He returned a moment later, with a stunned-looking Josh at his side.

"Are you two daftie?" Callum asked.

"I saw my mother," I said.

Josh still looked confused and shook his head to clear water from his eyes. He was susceptible to the song's power too and had probably seen a vision of his own that he wanted to follow.

"You saw a figment of your own imagination," Callum snapped. "You should know that by now. You know what that song does. What do you think happens to humans who try to find Hether Blether? They chase their desires deep into the ocean until they drown themselves."

I rolled my eyes. "We can't drown. We're finfolk, remember?"

"Not fully," Callum said, his eyes flashing angrily. "And that's what you keep forgetting. Your human side makes you susceptible to fatigue. Or maybe you would have kept following that vision long enough until you were lost. Being finfolk doesn't make you immortal."

I hated being scolded like a small child who had done a very bad thing. Josh seemed to recover quickly from the song's effects and now both of them looked like they expected me to swim off again at any moment, their bodies tensed.

"Fine," I snapped, turning away from them as I let a wave swoop me up and then drop me back down. "I'm sorry, okay? Let's get back in the boat and go."

"That would be a brilliant idea," Callum growled, "except the boat is gone."

I spun around, looking at the darkness around us. The three of us tread water in a small circle in the middle of the dark ocean. The boat had disappeared within the blackness around us. I couldn't see more than a couple feet in front of me.

Josh sighed. "Now what do we do?"

Callum lifted one hand from the water. He still gripped the twisted metal key. "We have the key. So we follow the song and swim."

Josh listened for a moment, then pointed. "It's

coming from that way."

Callum nodded. "Let's go."

* * *

The island appeared out of nowhere as the three of us swam and floated along the open black water. Thick fog swirled around us, obscuring the shape of the landmass, until my tail fin brushed sand and rocks below the surface.

At last, I could stand on my legs again, leaving my finfolk form behind as I waded toward shore. Josh splashed at my side, his jeans now tattered shreds attached to the waistband still around his hips. Neither of us had thought to grab our bags when we dove from the boat, so there were no extra clothes to change into. Josh's stony expression told me he had noticed this fact, even though he didn't say a word.

The beach was a mix of flat rocks and sand, but I collapsed onto the rough ground, trying to catch my breath. It had been a long swim and I wasn't sure how much time had passed. The faint hint of pink lit the eastern sky, signaling that it was almost dawn.

"Where's Callum?" Josh asked after a moment.

I sat up, looking back toward the water. I thought I could see the shape of his head still bobbing among the waves not far from shore. I cupped my hands around my mouth and shouted his name.

But he didn't seem to be moving any closer to the beach.

"What is he doing?" I grumbled. "Does he plan to swim back to Pierowall?"

"If this is Hether Blether, he may not be able to come ashore," Josh said. "He is banished."

"Where else does he expect to go?" I didn't want to dive back into the water after swimming for so long, but I didn't see any other option. I stalked into the crashing waves, letting the change overtake me as I swam toward Callum.

He tread water where the land began to rise up from the ocean. His face was pale in the early morning light and his breathing was ragged.

"What are you doing?" I asked. "Come ashore."

Callum shook his head. "I vowed not to set foot on the island when I left five years ago."

"So what do you plan to do? Stay out here forever?"

He looked over his shoulder, as if he expected the shores of Westray to materialize suddenly. When he turned back to me, his face still showed hesitation "If I come ashore, I'm subject to imprisonment," he said. "Or something worse."

I raised my eyebrows. "What did you do to get yourself banished anyway?"

Callum looked toward the beach, where Josh still waited in the darkness. He looked almost convinced to come ashore, but not quite.

"There is another problem aside from that," he said.

I sighed. "Which is?"

"My leg," Callum said. "The prosthetic came off while we swam. The current took it away before I could grab it."

Shame flooded my cheeks. I had forgotten about his leg. He was still able to swim, although he had lagged behind us.

It was my fault he didn't have his prosthetic anymore. Just like it was my fault that Josh and I didn't have our bags. And my fault that the boat was gone.

"I'll help you walk," I told him softly.

Callum regarded me warily. "Do you really think you can hold me up?"

"I'm stronger than I look," I snapped. "Besides, what other choice do you have other than hanging out here forever?"

Callum pressed his mouth into a tight line, but at last he turned toward the shore. I focused on the land and shed my finfolk form as I rose from the water, dripping and shivering in the cold air. I slipped Callum's left arm over my shoulders and my right arm around his waist to help steady him in the crashing waves. He wore a loose pair of khaki pants, which were still intact.

"You didn't change form," I said, my eyes widening.

Callum smirked. "I told you, I'm not finfolk anymore."

I shook my head. "You can't stop being finfolk."

"There is so much you don't know about our people," he told me.

Josh met us at the edge of the water. "Need help?"

he asked.

"I got him," I said, determined not to let anyone see how tired I already was from fighting the water as it rushed back against us. If this was penance for a foolish decision, I'd take it. It was another of a series of mistakes that had plagued my life.

I helped Callum ease onto a rock and then sat down next to him.

"So where are we?" Josh asked, looking around at the empty beach. The sand stretched behind us until it reached a thick grove of trees. There was no sign that the island was inhabited, no lights to lead the way and no one to meet us.

"Hether Blether," Callum said. "I expect we came ashore a few miles from the village. Which is a good thing."

"Why?" I asked.

"Because otherwise, the first greeting we would have had would have been at the end of a sentry's spear. Which still isn't out of the question."

"Where do we go from here?" Josh asked. "Which way is the village?"

Callum nodded toward his right. "That way. Beyond the forest, along the shore."

I yawned. My muscles ached and my eyelids drooped closed. A night of swimming and no sleep had left me on the brink of exhaustion.

"Can we take a nap first?" I asked.

Callum looked grim. "I don't think that's a good idea."

But I was already stretching out onto my back. "Just a few minutes. It won't do us any good to walk into the village exhausted. We need to be alert, right?" I closed my eyes, letting the warm feeling of sleep wash over me.

"We should get moving," Josh said. But he too sounded tired and I didn't hear any other protests as I finally fell into sleep.

Chapter 14

A sharp pain stabbed through my back and half-woke me from a deep sleep. I groaned and rolled over, squeezing my eyes shut at the morning light.

Whatever it was poked me again, this time harder and in the shoulder.

"Ow!" I pried my eyes open, staring up into the stern face of a man I didn't know. He wore a loose knee-length blue robe tied closed at the waist with an embroidered green belt, and a string of seashells hung around his neck. In his hands was a long stick, topped with a sharp, pointed piece of metal. Judging from the way it was pointed at me, it had to be what had woken me.

A quick glance around the beach showed that Josh was standing nearby, with a man in front of him also wielding a spear pointed at his chest. Callum still sat on the sand, but he was also being guarded.

"Get up," the man in front of me growled.

I clambered to my feet, brushing sand from my hands. "Who are you?" I asked.

"Sentries," Callum told me. The guard next to him poked his shoulder with his spear and Callum recoiled, scowling up at him. "I told you, I can't walk. Do you expect me to hop through the forest like a rabbit?"

The sentry scowled and then poked at Callum again. "Get up," he said.

I rushed toward Callum, pushing myself between him and the sentry. "He can't walk. Can't you see that?"

"They know, Sailor," Callum said. "They don't care because they know who I am."

"You should not have come back," the guard who had woken me said. "You know the sentence."

"Believe me, Artair, I'm not here because I want to be," Callum mumbled.

The guard, presumably Artair, glared even more, then pointed his spear at us. "Get up. This is the last time I will say it. After this, I will take care of you myself and save Domnall the trouble."

The look in the man's eyes showed he wasn't joking or making empty threats. I knelt and helped Callum to his feet, putting my arm around his waist again.

"He needs a prosthetic," I said as we started across the sand behind Artair. Josh fell into step next to us, and the other two guards took their places in the rear.

"He will not have need of a prosthetic much longer," Artair said, tossing the threat in his tone over his shoulder casually, as if he threatened to kill people every day. I gulped. Maybe around here, he did.

Artair led us away from the beach and into the trees, down a narrow path almost entirely overgrown. It would have been easy to miss for the untrained eye.

"Where are we going?" I whispered.

"To see Domnall, most likely," Callum answered. His body tensed under my hand, the muscles of his abdomen tight and twitching with each movement.

"Who is he?" I asked.

"The finfolk king," Callum said in a grim tone, as if the words were a death sentence.

The path wound through thick vegetation, and both Callum and I stumbled several times. At one point, his foot got caught in a vine on the ground. Of course none of the sentries offered help. Artair eyed us impatiently while Josh bent to free Callum's foot.

So far, finfolk weren't impressing me with their hospitality.

At last, we broke through the trees and came into a cleared stretch of beach. We stood at the bottom of sandy hills that rolled on into the distance around us. Small stone homes clustered together on the beach, parts of them immersed in the water that lapped onshore. A few larger buildings stood in the center of the village, including one that rose above the others and looked to be made of golden sand.

It was in that direction the sentries led us. A few

people—finfolk, I reminded myself—wandered through the village and they stopped to watch as we passed by. They all wore robes of different colors, both men and women, and they had long hair that they kept tied back. Most were curious, but some looked frightened. I heard one whisper Callum's name to someone else and then the word spread throughout the crowd. More people came out of homes and shops to peer at us, their wide eyes locked on Callum.

"This is...interesting," Josh muttered.

"Remember what I said," Callum whispered. "Don't let them know about your heritage. Use the Mooring name. It can protect you."

Something in Callum's tone and the fact that we were being escorted under armed guard made me wary to find out what would happen if these people knew that Josh and I were part human.

The building we were taken to looked almost like a castle, rising above the rest of the village. As we drew closer, I could see it was made of golden sandstone and rock, and almost blended into the earth around it. *A giant sandcastle,* I thought. Dried starfish and seahorses dotted the outside walls and a huge heavy door stood open to allow a sea breeze in.

Artair led us through the door and into a wide room. Tall windows stretched along the back wall, allowing light to stream in. Old, elaborately carved furniture was set throughout the room, heavy chairs and tables like I had seen in pictures of old castles. On the walls were paintings and woven tapestries, mixed with the wooden wheel from a ship and gleaming shields and swords.

A man stood near one window, outlined by the sunlight. He turned at the sound of our footsteps.

Artair paused and then bowed his head. "We found trespassers on the south side this morning. I believe you remember one of them."

The man's eyes never left Callum's as he stepped toward us. He had a scar across his face, from his right eye to his chin. Long blonde hair was left loose around his shoulders in wild waves.

"Callum," he growled. "Was I not clear what would become of you should you find your way back to this island?"

Callum didn't flinch at the tone in the man's voice. "You were," he said. "And yet, I came back anyway. I suppose that means you don't have the authority you like to believe you do after all."

The man I assumed to be Domnall, the finfolk king, stepped toward us, his face twisted into something sinister. His blue eyes flickered toward Callum's leg. "Perhaps you need to lose your other leg in order to remember what power I do have."

Callum stared back at him, his body tight against mine. I dug my nails into Callum's hand.

Finally, Domnall broke Callum's gaze and looked at Josh and then at me. "Who are you?" he demanded. "What business do you have here?"

"I'm Josh," my brother said, stepping forward. He swallowed a moment, then said, "Josh Mooring. And this is my sister Sailor." His voice didn't waver on the false name.

Domnall's eyebrows rose. "Mooring? You are finfolk."

It wasn't a question, but Josh nodded. "Yes. We've come in search of someone."

Domnall walked back to the table and picked up a dented metal cup. He took a sip, then said, "Your names are unknown to me. There is no one here you could possibly seek."

"We want to make sure," I said. "She left long ago and intended to come here. Her name was Coral Mooring."

I thought I saw Domnall flinch. It was only the slightest movement, so I couldn't be sure that he had. His still had the same stern expression when he turned back to me.

"There is no one here that you are looking for," he said. "Now the question is what to do with you. Because you accompany a known traitor and murderer, I am afraid I cannot let you go free until I am certain of your intentions."

My head whipped toward Callum, but he didn't meet my gaze. A traitor and *murderer?* My knees trembled, but I worried that if I let go of him I might fall.

"Take them upstairs," Domnall instructed Artair. "Make sure guards are posted outside of their room. They are not to leave this island."

"That went better than I'd hoped," Callum said once the heavy door had closed behind us. The three of us had been dumped into a narrow room that contained only a thin mattress on the floor and a chair near the slit that served as a window. The walls were stone and dark, the floor dusty and grainy with sand. The whole room had a wet feeling to it, almost like I was wading through water.

I whirled around to face him. "Better?" I asked. "We're prisoners."

"But we're unharmed," Callum responded, shrugging. "I'd call that better than the alternative."

I laughed, the sound bouncing off the walls around me. "I'm locked in a room on a vanishing island thousands of miles away from home. With a convicted murderer. And I'm supposed to be happy about that?" My voice rose in pitch as I spoke until I was nearly shrieking.

Josh put his hand on my shoulder. "We'll figure this out. We'll get out of here."

"Sure, we will," I snapped, pushing his hand away. "Once we're starving and shriveled up into nothing, we should all be able to squeeze through that window over there."

My voice broke on the last word. A lump choked me and tears stung my eyes. This wasn't how it was supposed to be. I was supposed to get here and find my mother, and she would be happy to see me. I wasn't supposed to be a prisoner in Hether Blether, still with no idea whether my mother had actually ever made it here.

I tried to hold the tears back, but they fell anyway. Then my chin quivered. A sob escaped from my mouth and I collapsed to the floor, burying my face in my hands so the guys wouldn't see.

Arms encircled me, hugging tight. Josh. I could recognize his scent anywhere. It wasn't the first time he'd held me while I'd cried. I didn't cry in front of people, except Josh. Even Dylan had never seen me break down like this.

Some time later, my shoulders stopped shaking and I sat up, wiping my eyes with the back of my hand. Josh still sat next to me, one arm draped around my shoulders.

"I didn't do it, by the way."

My gaze flicked toward Callum. He sat on the bed, his half leg extended across the mattress and his back pressed to the wall. I had almost forgotten he was there.

"What?" Josh asked him.

"In case you were wondering," he said, his eyes locked on mine, "I'm not a murderer."

"Then why do they think you are?" I asked.

Callum shrugged, his forehead creased into a deep scowl and his fists clenched in his lap. "Because they wanted someone to blame, and I was the easiest choice."

I looked at him for a long time, trying to figure out

if this was true. "What happened?" I asked.

But Callum turned his head, staring at the wall next to him.

We spent the entire day in that room. Food was delivered sometime during the afternoon, a tray of bread and fish. It wasn't much, not nearly enough for the three of us to share and feel full. But I ate every bit I had, then stared longingly at the food Callum had barely touched. I hadn't realized how hungry I was until the food arrived. If I closed my eyes, I could picture Grandma's cooking. Roast chicken and collards and steamed crabs and banana pudding. My stomach growled.

"Here." Callum pushed his plate toward me. He hadn't eaten enough to satisfy even a child.

I shook my head. "You should eat."

"I don't want it," he said. "Have it."

I felt guilty about the extra food, so I split it with Josh. Callum watched us eat, but he didn't look as if he regretted giving his meal away.

When I asked the guard outside for a bathroom break later, a metal pot was pushed through the door before it was slammed shut again.

"What's that?" I asked, wrinkling my nose at the pot.

"The toilet," Callum told me.

I looked at him like he'd lost his mind. "I am not peeing in that."

"Then don't," he said. "But could you bring it here so I can?"

I turned toward the door and pounded my fist on it. "Let me out!"

Chapter 15

It was easy to lose track of time, locked away in that little room. We slept a lot, since there wasn't much else to do. Josh studied the world outside through the narrow slit of a window on one wall, trying to gather information about Hether Blether. There wasn't much to see and his reports to us usually involved seeing finfolk swim along the shore to catch fish.

We were given robes to wear and food to eat, but that was the extent of our contact with anyone else. I was half-asleep when the door opened the guard called Artair stood there, his eyes scanning over the three of us. I sat up, my heart pounding against my ribs.

"You," he said, pointing at me. "Come with me."

Josh moved in front of me. "She doesn't go anywhere without me."

Artair barely glanced at him. "You were not requested. Domnall wants to speak to the girl."

A cold sweat broke out along my neck. What would Domnall want with me? I wasn't eager to see him again. I wasn't sure if I could hold back my anger at being imprisoned here.

"No," Josh insisted. "If she goes, I go with her."

Artair's grip on his spear tightened. He said in an even tone, "She will not be harmed. Domnall wants only to speak to her, and then she will be returned."

Josh opened his mouth to protest again. I glanced at Callum, who nodded slightly to me. His eyes told me it would be okay. I had no choice but to trust him.

"It's okay," I told Josh, pushing him back. "I'll be fine."

"You don't have to go," Josh said in a low voice.

I waved his words away, trying to hide the nervousness I felt. "I'll be back soon."

Artair led me back through the same narrow halls I had traveled down on my way toward the room where we were being kept. How long ago had that been?

"How long have we been here?" I asked.

I didn't expect Artair to answer me, but he responded, "Two days."

Two days? It had felt like a week, at least. I had no sense of time within my prison. I wasn't even sure that time on a vanishing island worked the same as it did in the rest of the world.

Instead of taking me to the large room where I had first met Domnall, Artair delivered me to a small room downstairs. The room was nicely decorated, the walls painted with blue lines that I could see were meant to be waves. The chairs in this room were gathered around a large door cut into the floor, which was closed. White marble statues stood in the corners of the room, depicting men and women and one of a small bronze mermaid. All of them had blank expressions, empty eyes and frozen smiles. Something about the statues disturbed me, so I kept my gaze away from them.

Large windows along one wall looked out over water that glimmered under the hazy sun. Crystal prisms hung in front of the windows, casting little rainbows all over the room. I reached for one, turning it slowly in my hand so I could see the colors inside it. Grandma had crystals hanging from the skylights in our house back home. Sometimes we would lay on the floor under them and watch the rainbows dancing on the walls.

We hadn't done that in years. One day I stopped doing it, and eventually Grandma stopped asking.

"It is a beautiful view," said a voice behind me.

I jumped and found Domnall standing near a chair. He hadn't been there when I'd entered the room.

He gestured toward the chair across from him. "Please sit. Would you like something to drink?"

I was desperately thirsty, so I took the cup of water Domnall offered. I considered the idea that it might have been tainted with something—a poison to get rid of me, maybe. But it tasted like saltwater, nothing more.

"Thanks," I said grudgingly.

Domnall sat down, keeping his back straight and regal, his hands cupping his own drink. "I am sorry that your welcome to Hether Blether has been...unpleasant. It was for safety concerns, I assure you."

"What do I need protection from?" I asked.

"Not your protection," he corrected me. "I was concerned for my people."

I scowled. "I have no interest in your people. The only reason I'm here is to look for my mother."

Domnall took a sip of his own drink, then set the glass down on an old wooden table next to his chair. "You must have come a long way," he said.

I nodded. "Yeah. So?"

"Where exactly are you from?"

A chill crept its way down my back, making the little hairs along my arms stand on end. "Why do you want to know?" I asked.

He smoothed the fabric of his robe across his lap. "I am only curious. It is not often a lost one such as yourself comes back to Hether Blether."

"Lost one?"

"That is what we call those descended from the finfolk who left our island many years ago," he explained. "Truthfully, the stories have become mostly legend. It was always believed that anyone who had actually left most likely met their demise somewhere in the human world." He leaned forward, resting his elbows on his knees. "But *you*. You are proof that there are finfolk out there, lost ones still living through their descendents. It is a remarkable thing to consider, a colony of finfolk far from our shores. You must understand how fascinated that makes me."

He spoke with the smoothness of someone who was used to charming people. It was no wonder that he was king.

But I also had experience in charming people. And I knew lies and half-truths when I heard them.

"What makes you think there are all these others out there? Maybe I'm the last of my people."

Domnall scratched his whiskers for a moment. The long scar across his face formed a dividing line within the hair across his jaw. "How old are you?"

That question seemed general enough. "Sixteen," I told him.

"Where did you come from?"

"Across the ocean," I answered vaguely.

"Where?" he asked again.

I waved a hand. "Far away."

He scowled down at me, but I clenched my teeth to keep my chin from quivering.

"How many others like you are there?" he asked.

"None."

He blinked. "None? I assume you have parents, a family. You have a brother, so there is at least one other like you."

I raised my chin. "There are none like me. I'm one of a kind."

His forehead creased into an annoyed scowl. Whatever it was he wanted, I wasn't playing his game the way he had expected. Every muscle in my body was tensed, ready to spring into action at the first sign of trouble.

My gaze fell on Domnall's hands. They were huge, each one more than half the size of my head. I knew I couldn't outmatch him physically if he decided he'd had enough of me. My only hope was that maybe my smaller body was faster than his larger one.

"How do you know Callum?" he asked.

I blinked, surprised at the change in questioning. "I met him in Westray."

"How much of his past has he told you?"

"Not much," I said honestly. "He told us he was banished. He didn't even intend to come here. He was only going to get us close, and then he planned to go back to Westray. But then the boat was lost because I —"

I stopped myself in time, remembering Callum's warning. If I mentioned that I had seen my mother because of the song, they would know I wasn't fully finfolk.

Domnall raised his eyebrows. "Because?"

"Because we heard the song and jumped into the water to follow it." I shrugged. "Callum apparently couldn't resist the call."

Domnall sat back in his seat, a skeptical look on his face. He studied me intently, as if he could find the answers he wanted written on my body. His stare was becoming unnerving and I shifted a little in my seat.

"Why are you asking me so many questions?" I asked. "I told you why I'm here. I want to find my mother. Then I'll go and you can forget all about me."

He stood and moved toward the window, his back to me.

"How would you like a more comfortable living arrangement?" he asked. "You can move out of that room you are in. You will be free to explore the island all you want."

I narrowed my eyes. "What about my brother and Callum?"

Domnall's shoulders tensed, but he said, "Your brother too. Callum...I will need to consider his case. He is a convicted criminal here. But I will see what I can do to make sure he is treated well."

I suspected that all Domnall had to do was say the word and the charges against Callum could disappear entirely. A king had the ultimate power, didn't he?

"What's the catch?" I asked.

"No *catch*, as you say," Domnall said. "I want you to be treated well during your stay here. I would like to get to know you, Sailor."

There had to be something else, something I wasn't seeing.

"No deal," I said. "I'll rot in that room, thanks."

I got up to leave, assuming that our little talk was over now that I'd turned him down. But then Domnall turned to me, his hands clasped behind his back. The sunlight streaming through the window shone on his golden hair. He was handsome, even with the jagged scar marring his face.

"What if," he said slowly, "I could take you to your mother?"

Chapter 16

Josh lunged at me when I entered the room. "What happened? Are you okay?"

"I'm fine," I said. I swallowed hard, then added, "We're free to go."

Josh stepped back, looking at me and then at Artair, who stood in the hall, his spear still in his hand. "What?"

"We're being moved," I said, not quite meeting Josh's eyes. "We're not prisoners anymore."

"Moved to where?" Callum spoke up. He still sat on the mattress, unmoving, but he eyed me suspiciously

"Domnall is giving us a suite to stay in here at the palace."

"But why would they lock us in here, just to let us go like that?" Josh asked, narrowing his eyes. "What happened in there?"

The room was silent for a moment. I didn't want to tell them I had agreed to talk to Domnall in exchange for seeing my mama, despite the fact that he scared me. Josh might have understood, but I doubted Callum would.

"Nothing happened," I said at last. "Domnall realized there was no valid reason to keep us locked up."

Callum snorted, but I ignored him.

"If you do not wish to be captive any longer, I suggest you come along," Artair said from the doorway.

Josh studied me a moment longer, then he turned toward Callum. But I grabbed his arm and shook my head.

"What?" Josh asked, his forehead creased into a deep scowl.

"It's just us," I said softly.

"Just us what?"

My gaze met Callum's for the briefest moment. His green eyes turned dark and then he said, "She means Domnall is only releasing the two of you. I get to stay here, enjoying the comforts of these lovely quarters."

"Sailor?" Josh asked, a sharp tone to his voice.

"I'm sorry," I whispered "I tried, but..."

"But I'm a criminal," Callum finished when my voice trailed off. He waved a hand at us. "Go. Don't worry about me. I imagine I'll be right here for some time, unless Domnall decides to toss me off the island again."

Every part of me rebelled at the idea of leaving Callum locked away. But there was nothing I could do. Domnall had armed sentries everywhere. I couldn't possibly hope to escape with Callum unnoticed, and not having his prosthetic made it impossible for him to outrun them.

"We can't leave him," Josh said. "He helped us get here."

"We have to." I pulled Josh toward the door.

The last image I had of Callum was of him sitting on the bed, his face turned toward the narrow window slit. He looked as if he had accepted his fate long ago, but something inside me lurched with fear.

"I'll come back soon," I said.

Callum didn't acknowledge my words.

Artair led us to a wing of the palace on the lower level. He opened a set of heavy wooden doors to reveal a room suspended over the beach. A door cut into the center of the floor showed waves lapping onshore underneath the suite. The furniture was situated near the hole, chairs and tables gathered around it as if the hole in the floor were a wide-screen TV.

"There are two bedrooms," Artair said, gesturing toward doors along one wall. "A conch will sound at meal times. Domnall usually eats alone in his quarters, but you may eat in the dining hall. You are free to come and go as you please." The quick scowl that flashed across Artair's face showed he didn't particularly like that idea. "The village can provide you with anything you need, but please do not call attention to yourselves. I trust you will not cause any problems for our people."

With that, Artair left without even saying good-bye. He shut the door behind him and Josh and I were alone in the small suite, listening to the sound of the water under our feet.

"Tell me what happened," Josh demanded. "I want to know everything from the time you left to see Domnall until we ended up here."

"I told you, nothing happened." I walked over to a cabinet and pulled it open. Inside, dishes sat in neat stacks. They were old metal plates, etched with swirling designs. Silver cups rimmed with flaking gold lined an upper shelf. I pulled a cup down and inspected it. It looked like something from an old movie. A cup a king in an ancient castle may have used.

Josh crossed his arms. "Something must have, or else we'd still be in that room with Callum. What did Domnall want?"

"He asked a few questions," I said. "He wanted to know where we had come from."

Josh's eyes narrowed. "What did you tell him?"

"I didn't tell him about Swans Landing," I said. "I told him we came from across the ocean, that's all."

"And?"

I scowled. "And what?"

"And how exactly did you earn his goodwill and get us into this suite?"

I gripped the back of a chair, digging my nails into

the wood. "What exactly are you implying, Josh?"

"I've seen the way you constantly throw yourself at Dylan Waverly to get what you want. For all I know, that's how you convinced Callum to bring us here. So what exactly did Domnall get from you that made him release us?"

I darted across the room, my hand smacking across Josh's cheek with a loud crack. "I haven't done anything except save your life," I said through clenched teeth.

"What about Callum's life?" Josh asked. His cheek was already beginning to turn bright red, but he stared back at me unflinching. "Can you live with yourself in this cozy little suite while he sits in that room alone?"

"I tried to get him out," I said. "Domnall wouldn't agree to it! For all we know, Callum did kill someone. We don't know him any better than anyone else here. How can we be sure we can trust him?"

"He hasn't given us a reason not to," Josh said.

I turned away from him, blinking back the tears that stung my eyes. I had tried to get Callum out of there. It wasn't my fault Domnall wouldn't listen to my arguments. What else was I supposed to do?

"I'm going to take a nap," I said. "Tomorrow I have to meet with Domnall again."

"Why?" Josh asked.

I leaned back against the wall, sighing as the little energy left in my body drained away. I almost couldn't say the words, couldn't believe they might be real

"Because he's going to take me to my mama."

Chapter 17

Josh's snores drifted to me through the wall separating our rooms. At least someone was getting some sleep. I rolled over again, staring at the faint slivers of moonlight spilled across the bed. The mattress was too firm, the sheet too scratchy, and my room too cold.

But I knew all of that wasn't what kept me up. My body bordered on exhaustion, but my mind was wide awake.

Was I wrong to leave Callum locked in that room? Was he okay? And where exactly was my mother? Domnall hadn't told me anything except that he could take me to her. Part of me was terrified Domnall would take me to a grave. I didn't even know if finfolk buried their dead or tossed them out to sea, but I prayed I wouldn't find out anytime soon.

Early the next morning, a knock sounded on the door of the suite before it opened. Artair stepped back to allow Domnall passage into the room. He looked as towering and imposing as he had the day before, though he had tied his wild blonde hair back.

His eyes scanned the room, before settling on Josh and me. We sat at the table, eating fruits Josh had taken from the kitchen. Well, Josh was eating. I hadn't managed more than a couple of bites of berries.

"Come," Domnall said, gesturing toward me.

Josh stood with me and Domnall paused to look back at him. "I made my deal with your sister only," he said. "You may wait here if you wish."

Josh set his jaw and stared back at the older man. "Where Sailor goes, I go."

Irritation flashed across Domnall's face. "I assure you, your sister will not be harmed. You have my word."

Josh laughed. "Your word doesn't mean much to me."

I didn't want Josh to say anything else that would get him into trouble, so I stepped between them. "I'll be back as soon as I can," I said in a low voice. "I'll tell you everything that happens."

He scowled and then turned away. "Fine. Do what you want."

I followed Domnall without looking back at Josh. He would be angry for a while, but he'd get over it.

To my surprise, Domnall led me away from the village. We followed the shoreline through brush and rolling hills, until we reached a narrow strip of beach. The water was calmer here than it had been where we'd come ashore a few days ago. A long, slender boat made of a pale wood bobbed on the surface.

Domnall gestured toward the boat. "After you."

I narrowed my eyes. "Where are you taking me?"

"Not far." He pointed into the distance to our left, where I could see the shape of land. "It is a peninsula that juts off from the island. We could walk there, but the bay is quicker."

I let him help me into the boat and then he followed, sitting down on a wooden seat near the bow. I sat on the seat behind him, and then Artair pushed us off from the shore. He expertly jumped into the boat, not even rocking it slightly. Then he rested his spear in the floor and replaced it with a long, slender double-sided oar.

The breeze lifted my hair around my head and I had to keep pushing it out of the way so I could see the peninsula as we drew across the water. The bay was clear here, almost a brilliant green. I could see fish and small sharks, even crabs and starfish moving across the sand under the boat. The water was so shallow I could reach down to touch the bottom if I wanted. It felt peaceful here.

It took me a moment to realize the peace I felt was because my body didn't feel pulled between land and sea. We floated several yards offshore and yet I could feel both the water and the earth vibrating evenly inside me. I had never felt this kind of peace in my life.

When we reached the peninsula, Artair expertly guided the boat to a small dock that jutted into the water. He helped Domnall and me onto the dock, then he returned to the boat. Domnall offered me his arm and led me up the cobblestone path to a group of wooden homes.

I glanced over my shoulder at Artair, who sat in the boat with his face turned toward the water. "Isn't he coming?" I asked.

"He will stay with the boat," Domnall said. "I asked him for privacy."

A chill prickled across my scalp at the idea of being alone with Domnall, far from Josh. He must have sensed my anxiety because he added, "As I said, your safety is assured."

A miniature village sat along the peninsula, a group of seven homes all situated in a semi-circle. Behind the homes, the water sparkled in the morning sun.

But the tranquility of the scenery didn't extend to the village itself. The peninsula seemed abandoned. Some cottages sat half-buried in the surf that lapped against the shore, the wood wet and crumbling under a coating of sea lichen. Black windows stared at us and doors gaped open in a silent scream.

I shivered. "What is this place?"

"It was once another village on the island," Domnall said. At my surprised look, he smiled slightly. "The main village was not always the only inhabited place here. Once we lived all over the island, and others around it. But now..." He let his words hang in the air, unspoken.

No one came out to greet us as we approached the homes, but Domnall seemed to know exactly where he wanted to go. He passed by a few empty houses, until finally, he paused at one and nodded to me.

The house looked the same as the others, except this one had something carved into the wood of the door. I stepped closer and lifted my fingers to trace the image. A lily. Lily was my mama's middle name, and mine as well. I placed my hand on the knob and sucked in a deep breath, trying to prepare myself for what I would see on the other side.

The room was small, the walls a pale sandstone. A simple bed took up most of the room, covered with a frayed blue quilt. In front of the window stood a table that served as a desk, covered with books and papers.

And in a chair at the desk sat a woman. She was too thin. I could see the bones of her shoulder blades poking through her robe, which hung off her, threatening to slip down one skeletal shoulder. She was bent over the desk, concentrating on the lines she drew on the paper in front of her. Her hair wasn't the brilliant gold it was in Grandma's photo albums, but a dull shade of graying blonde that fell in greasy locks around her shoulders.

My mouth had gone dry. I swallowed, scraping my sandpaper tongue against my teeth. "Mama?" I asked, my voice almost a squeak.

For a moment, she didn't acknowledge me. Then she turned, looking over her shoulder. Her face was hollow, her eyes sunken and lined with dark circles. Lines etched the skin around her tight mouth and her cheeks hung from her bones. There was no spark of recognition in her eyes.

I tried to fight the urge to run to her, to throw my arms around her and burst into tears. Here she was at last. My mama and I were in the same room, she was so close I could reach out and touch her.

"I don't want anything to eat right now," she said after a moment. Then she turned back to her papers.

I stood there, trying to make sense of her words. Hadn't she heard what I'd said?

I stepped closer, reaching out a trembling arm to touch her shoulder, but then pulled it back before I did.

"Mama?" I said again. "It's me. It's Sailor."

She blinked at me. I stared into her blue eyes, searching for anything that would let me know she knew who I was.

Her eyes lit up and my heart skipped a beat. "My Sailor. So small, so perfect. He would have loved her." Her smile faded and her chin quivered.

Was she talking about Oliver Canavan, Josh's and my father?

"Mama?" I said again. "I'm here. It's Sailor. I came to find you."

Mama shook her head, but her expression still had a faraway look, as if she didn't hear me. "Sailor is at home, with her grandmother," she said. "It's better this way. It will all be better."

"Mama," I said again, trying to keep my voice even,

"I'm here. It's time to come home. I'll take you back."
I was aware of Domnall's presence in the doorway and I sucked in a steadying breath. I didn't want him to know how I was crumbling inside.

Mama turned back to her drawings. "I have to leave the island," she said. She shuffled the papers together into a messy stack. "I have to go. I have to save them."

"Save who?" I asked.

But my mother kept stacking her papers, not even paying attention to me. "I have to find it," she said. Her voice rose higher and higher as she spoke. "I promised. It will all be better when I go."

Suddenly she reached out, grasping my hand tight in hers. Her eyes were wide and panicked. "Everything will be okay. Right?"

She looked so lost, so scared. Tears burned in my eyes, but I nodded. "Everything will be okay," I said.

She relaxed, letting go of my hand and turning back to her desk. She unstacked her papers and set them in front of her. "Everything will be okay," she echoed.

It felt like the conversation had come to an end. My mother turned her attention back to her drawings, leaving me to look at her sloping back.

I backed out of the room, pulling the door shut. My hands clenched into fists at my sides and I shuddered as I took a deep breath.

"You knew?" I asked in a hoarse whisper. I didn't turn to look at Domnall. "You knew she was...like that?"

"She has been like that since I found her on the

beach sixteen years ago," he said.

Something lodged deep in my throat, a burning ache that wouldn't go away no matter how many times I swallowed. "And you didn't think to tell me before I..." I paused, trying to regain my composure. "You didn't think I should know before I walked in there?"

I glared up at him. He didn't look surprised or concerned. The scar on his face cut across his skin, leaving a jagged line that never moved.

"Would you have still wanted to see her if you had known what would be waiting for you in there?" he asked.

"She's my mother," I said.

"She is broken," Domnall told me. "We keep her here to protect her."

"She needs help. She doesn't need to be hidden away in this ghost town. Does anyone else know she's here?"

Domnall took a few steps, his gaze roaming over the decrepit homes. "This was once a beautiful village." He reached out to pull a young bud from a tree, twirling the green leaves between his fingers. "Not only finfolk lived here. There were humans, as well."

My eyes widened. "You have humans here?"

Domnall sneered as he shook his head. "Not anymore. The last of them died many years ago. Now this is a home for those who are lost."

"How many others like her have there been?"

"A few, here and there over the years," Domnall told me. "All of them sick in some way. They stay here until they pass on or return to the sea. We keep them away from the rest of the people here because their presence would only raise questions for which we do not yet have the answers. Your mother is the only one still here. I was not certain the woman we had here was your mother, until I came to see her myself two days ago. When I mentioned your name to her, she became agitated, like she did today."

There was still so much I needed to know. I had come so far, only to find her like this.

"What happened to her?" I asked.

Domnall stepped closer, leaning down slightly so we were more at eye level. "Humans did this," he said in a soft voice. "This is the effect they have on our people."

I swallowed, clenching my fists tight at my sides.

"They destroy what makes us finfolk. They make us live in fear, ashamed of who we are. You know this. You have seen it."

Memories flashed before my eyes. Elizabeth Connors and her friends, laughing as they tormented me again and again. Sneers shot my way in the hall, being pushed into lockers, mashed potatoes crushed into my hair in the cafeteria. Dylan at my side, continually telling me to ignore it all, even though I wanted to explode and make them all as miserable as they tried to make me.

Yes, I knew what humans were capable of doing to us.

But I was also part human and the two sides of me

battled for control of my thoughts.

"They are killing our people," Domnall told me. "We once thought they were good for us. We kept some of them here as toys, trinkets from the outside world. But they poisoned our land. When they mated with our people, they introduced a weakness we had not expected. We learned our lesson too late. Their influence is spreading and killing the mists that keep us from their sight. Soon, we will no longer remain hidden. They will find us and they will take this island as they have taken our homes before."

Domnall's blue eyes looked back at me, his face soft and open. "I need your help to save us. To keep everyone from becoming like your mother."

"How?" I asked.

"Hether Blether needs its people back in order to survive. Tell me where your people are," he said in a soothing tone. "I can bring them home."

"What good can we do? My people don't even know for sure that this place exists."

Domnall ran a hand over my head, smiling tenderly. "You have more magic inside you than you know, Sailor Mooring."

"Finfolk aren't magical," I said.

He laughed. "Do you think the song is only meant to call us home? We speak the essence of the water and earth. We can manipulate them and the beings created from them to our will."

I couldn't imagine Grandma ever willingly leaving Swans Landing. Even a part of me missed the island

and wanted to go back.

"No," I said in a firm voice. "I'm not telling you where the others are."

Domnall's expression was kind and gentle as he reached for my hand. "Sailor, please understand we are only trying to help you. Help *all* of you. We want everyone to live healthy, peaceful lives. You can do that here. This is a safe place."

His fingers were icy cold when they touched mine and I jerked back from his grasp. Despite his reassuring words, something about this place didn't feel safe at all.

"Thank you for bringing me to my mother," I told him.

I pushed past him and hurried down the path, back toward the dock where Artair waited.

If my mama was the only living lost finfolk here besides Josh and me, what exactly had happened to the others who'd left Swans Landing?

Chapter 18

"Maybe I should talk to her," Josh said. He squatted in the sand on the part of the beach directly under our suite. The large door in the floor gaped open above us, and a rope ladder hung down to allow us access in and out. Josh kept his gaze focused on the approaching water as he spoke. His hand shot out as the tide rolled in, sending a splash up around him. "Damn," he muttered when he came up empty-handed.

Josh had been trying to catch small fish that became trapped in the tide pool he had created, which he would then use as bait for larger fish. While I'd been visiting my mother, he had spent the morning carving a homemade fishing pole from a long stick and an old piece of string he'd found in the cabin.

Josh didn't like being indebted to Domnall for food,

and so he had come up with a plan to catch food for us. Apparently, this involved the human way of catching fish with a pole and bait.

"She doesn't know where she is," I reminded him. Mama had seemed so empty, so hollow and unfocused. A part of me wished I had never come here and had never found her. Shame flooded through me at those thoughts. She was my mother, and I couldn't leave her here for the rest of her life.

"She wouldn't be able to answer any questions," I went on. "She barely even knows her own name."

A group of finfolk swam in the water nearby, only a few yards down the beach. They jumped among the waves before disappearing under the surface. They had given us curious looks before entering the water about half an hour before, but none had dared come close. I wondered what the finfolk of Hether Blether thought about us outsiders. We didn't look any different than they did, but it was obvious we were not a part of their world.

"You said she's confused about past and present," Josh pointed out. "She may very well remember what happened the night our dad died. She may be able to tell us what we need to know."

Did Josh ever stop thinking about himself? All he cared about was getting answers to his questions.

"What she needs is to go home," I snapped. "She doesn't need to be locked away in that little shack."

Josh looked at me over his shoulder. "Do you honestly think she could swim that far?"

I crossed my arms and turned away from him, watching the clouds glide across the gray sky.

"If she could remember that night," Josh said, "we could have our answers."

"You mean, *you* could have your answers," I snapped. "I don't care about anything other than getting my mama home."

Josh didn't look at me as he said, "He was your father too. You should be at least a little curious to know how he died."

Biologically, Oliver Canavan was my father, but he had never been more than a name to me. I'd had no photos of him, not like the ones of my mother that I'd poured over so many times while growing up. I had no stories that anyone had told me about him. The only thing I knew was he had been married to another woman, fell in love with my mama, and then drowned.

He might have been Josh's daddy, but I had no claim to him.

"I don't want to bother her with questions that might upset her," I said at last. "We're not going to ask about that night until she gets better."

A shout nearby caught our attention. The finfolk that had gone out to swim had gathered together in a group, bobbing among the waves. They shouted to each other, waving others still lingering farther away to come close.

As we watched, the finfolk waded toward shore, already shedding their fin form. They carried a woman between them, her head limp against her chest. Bright red blood trickled in rivulets down her tail fin from a long gash where her skin met blue-green scales. The woman didn't change form as they carried her onto the beach and she didn't respond to their shouts.

I followed Josh closer to the group. They didn't look at us as we approached. Everyone bent over the woman, all eyes on her still limp shape on the sand.

"Caileigh," a man said in a throaty voice, looking toward an older woman. "She's been bit."

The woman nodded as she pushed a lock of wet gray hair from her lips. She closed her eyes, placing one hand on the injured woman's stomach.

A low hum filled the air around us. It was a finfolk song like I had never heard before. The other voices of the group joined in, humming louder and deeper. I waited for the visions of my mama that always came when I heard the song, but nothing happened other than a vibration that filled my body with energy.

"They're using both songs," Josh whispered at my side. He didn't tear his gaze away from the group. "The songs of earth and water in one."

He was right. I could hear and feel the notes of both songs, but they were combined into a melody I'd never known was possible. In Swans Landing, we rarely used the earth songs and I'd never heard of anyone mixing it with a water song.

The song grew louder, drumming in my ears and making me gasp for deep breaths. Gold bursts sparkled at the sides of my vision. I felt alive and strong

On the sand, all of the finfolk had their hands on the

woman. She writhed, moaning, as her body changed from finfolk to human. The scales dissolved into skin, her tail fin sliding back into place as toes. The gash in her side changed too. As her body remade itself, the skin fused together, closing up as neatly as if it had never been torn. Only the red smear of bloody water on her skin remained as evidence.

When the song ended, the woman sat up. "I am well," she assured her friends, giving them a grateful smile.

The finfolk helped her to her feet. She swayed unsteadily a moment, but then seemed to be perfectly healed.

My heartbeat pounded in my ears as the effects of the song still lingered within me. I stepped forward.

"How did you do that?" I asked.

The finfolk turned toward me, their heads whipping my way at my question. We looked at each other for a long moment, no one daring to move.

Their gazes flickered toward the palace behind us and then they turned back to the water, diving in without another word.

I turned to Josh. "Did you see that?"

He nodded, his eyes wide. "I didn't know anything like that was possible."

Tingles of excitement flooded through me. "If the songs can be used to heal, maybe I can do it for my mother and fix whatever is wrong with her."

Why hadn't we thought of this before? Back home, we used a water song to help new finfolk transition between forms with less pain. The songs could be used for comfort, so why not healing? Since we were connected to both land and water as finfolk, the two songs combined together spoke to both parts of our souls. It made so much sense.

But Josh looked doubtful. "I'm sure if that could be done, Domnall has already tried it."

I clenched my fists at my sides. "We don't know that. This might be what she needs to make her better."

"And what if she never gets better?" Josh asked quietly.

His question sent a chill through me and I gritted my teeth together.

"She will," I told him. "She has to."

Chapter 19

"Mama?"

She sat in the dry grass near her cottage, her dull hair blowing in the breeze. She faced the sparkling water that surrounded the peninsula, her lips curled into a small smile.

My mother didn't turn as I approached, so I sat down next to her, my movements slow to keep from startling her. As I crossed my legs, I realized she was humming softly as she sat there. I cocked my head, listening to the melody of her song.

It was familiar, but it wasn't a finfolk song. It was a church hymn, one I'd heard many times in the Swans Landing Fellowship Church. Grandma used to make me go when I was a kid. The other people—the humans—didn't like our presence there, so we'd always come in a few minutes late, sit in the back pew, and leave a few minutes early to avoid stares.

"Do you remember Swans Landing, Mama?" I asked softly.

Mama shifted in the grass, smiling wide. "It's going to be a beautiful summer," she said, her eyes still on the water. "It's always exciting when the tourists start coming, especially the new people. We all pretend to be ordinary, like them." Her smile faded a little. "It's fun to pretend I could be like them. Able to go anywhere I wanted."

Her words surprised me. From all the stories I'd heard about my mama and the pictures I'd seen, she'd always seemed so happy in her life on the island. I had always thought the only reason she'd left was because of my daddy's death and what happened after between the humans and finfolk.

"You wanted to leave Swans Landing?" I asked.

"I told him I want to see everything there is to see in the world," Mama said. "He promised he'd take me one day." She frowned and looked down at her hands. "But that's impossible."

Something sharp twisted in my stomach. She must have been talking about my daddy and the plans they had made together. I tried to picture them, sitting on the beach back in Swans Landing, planning out a life together they would never get the chance to have.

I had to try to make her better. I hated seeing her like this, stuck inside her own head.

"Mama," I said, turning so I faced her in the grass.

"I'm going to try something, okay? All you need to do is sit here and listen."

I reached toward her, but drew my hand back when she flinched.

"It's okay," I assured her. "I won't hurt you. I need to hold your hand for a minute."

Moving very, very slowly, I slipped my hand around her bony one. Her fingers were twigs in my grasp, her skin cold and papery thin.

I closed my eyes and focused on the vibrations of the earth under me and the water nearby. I pulled the essences of both into me as I took a deep breath.

I started with a few notes of the water song since I knew it better. Then I focused on pulling in the earth song too.

My hum cracked, the notes feeling raw and wrong in my throat. I coughed, then tried again.

Sweat trickled down my forehead as I focused on the two opposing songs. The finfolk on the beach had made it look so easy. But the songs were so different from each other, it was difficult to combine them in a way that made them work together while still being separate. I managed to make them merge for only a few notes, but I couldn't hold the song very long.

After a several long minutes of trying, I opened my eyes. The world spun around me and I wanted to sink back into the grass to take a nap.

Mama still sat at my side, staring out into the water. She didn't seem to notice my exhaustion.

"Mama?" I asked.

I knew it was useless to hope, but a part of me still held onto the tiny fragment of hope that maybe something I'd done had worked.

Mama smiled. "It's going to be a beautiful summer," she said.

* * *

Artair stood on the beach near where the rowboat was docked, his back to me. He didn't turn, even though my footsteps crunching on the sand and broken shells announced my arrival. Thankfully, Domnall had been busy and unable to come with us on this trip to the peninsula and I'd managed to convince Josh to stay behind, so it was just the tall sentry and me.

"I expect your visit went well," Artair said when I reached him.

I cast a glare his way. "Let's go," I grumbled.

He held out a hand to help me into the boat, but I ignored him and climbed in, nearly falling overboard when the boat rocked unexpectedly. The narrow finfolk boat was unlike anything I was used to back home and it made me feel like I'd never had my sea legs.

Artair sat down, boarding the boat with a fluid movement that didn't cause even the tiniest sway. He picked up the oars and began rowing, pulling us away from the peninsula, away from my mother.

It had been a wasted effort, as Josh thought it would be. I hated going back to the palace to tell him he was right. Maybe Domnall had already tried to use the songs on my mother and they hadn't worked.

"Why do you insist on being unhappy here?"

I raised my eyebrows at Artair. "What?"

"This is the finfolk homeland," he told me. "You belong here. Yet, you look as if you would rather go back to the human world. You do not try to find happiness here."

I crossed my arms. "You wouldn't understand. This is the only place you've ever lived, isn't it?"

"It is the only place I have ever been meant to belong," Artair said. "I have no interest in going anywhere else. What would there be for me in the human world, other than sickness and pain?"

"It's not all bad," I said. "There are good things. TV and movies. Surfing."

He wrinkled his nose. "I do not know what those things are, but here in Hether Blether, we have everything we need."

"Don't you ever get bored with it?" I asked. "Don't you ever wish you could go somewhere else, see something new?"

Artair was quiet for a moment as he rowed, deep lines etched across his forehead. He was at least fifteen years older than me, maybe more. I hadn't really looked hard at him before now, but away from the palace, he looked different. Softer.

"My family is here," he said at last. "All of my family, back for many generations, have walked these shores and swam in these waters. It is where we belong. It is our home, and it is my duty to protect it."

"You can't survive cut off from the rest of the world forever," I told him. "There are, what? A few hundred finfolk here. You'll die out eventually if you don't introduce new people to the group."

"But that is what Domnall is trying to do," Artair said. He stopped rowing, resting his elbows on his knees as he leaned toward me. "If you would tell us where your people are, we could bring them back here and increase the finfolk population. We could ensure the survival of our species."

I clamped my mouth shut, lips pressed tight. Had Artair planned this all along to try to get me to tell him about Swans Landing? He was Domnall's soldier, I had to remember that. Everything Artair did was at Domnall's command or for his benefit.

I scowled at him before turning my face toward the village on the other side of the bay. "Take me back to the palace," I demanded.

Chapter 20

Domnall stood as we entered the dining room, beaming at us. "Thank you for joining me," he said in a pleasant tone. He was dressed nicely, in a gray-green robe the color of the ocean. His hair was loose and shining all around his shoulders. Even the scar on his face didn't stand out as much, so he looked regal and handsome, like a king in a fairy tale.

The table before him was already full of fruits and fish and breads displayed in gleaming silver trays. My stomach roiled at the sight of more fish. I was so sick of eating fish, I'd do almost anything for a pizza or a cheeseburger.

Domnall pulled out a chair for me on his left and I sat. Josh took the seat across from me. The table was so full I expected more people to join us, but then

Domnall sat and filled his plate from the bowls on the table.

"Eat," he said, smiling again.

Josh and I exchanged a look. After a moment, Josh began filling his plate.

I studied the dish in front of me. The plate was painted with a picture of a large ship and the date 1850 etched along the bottom. The gold bands etched into the rim were expertly done and looked expensive.

"Do the finfolk make these dishes?" I asked.

Domnall gave me an amused smile. "The dishes are given to us by the sea. These are some of the finer pieces we have found."

Josh paused, his fork halfway to his mouth. "You find them?"

"On our beaches and in our waters."

Josh's eyes widened. "You mean, from shipwrecks, don't you?"

Domnall waved a hand. "I do not know their origin, only that the sea brings them to us. We take almost everything we need from the sea."

I gulped, imagining the humans on a doomed ship who had once used the plate that now sat in front of me. I scanned over the tapestries on the walls, the shields and swords displayed as art, the unseeing statues tucked away in the corners of the palace. These were human creations, stolen from the outside world and brought to Hether Blether.

"Eat," Domnall urged me.

For a moment, I considered the idea that this might

be a trap of some sort. Maybe the food was poisoned so Domnall could get rid of us easily. But he ate the same food we did and when he took a bite without falling over dead, I figured it must have been safe. For now.

"I trust you are enjoying your stay in Hether Blether," Domnall said. "Your suite is suitable for your needs?"

"Yes," Josh said. "Thank you for everything."

"Where is Callum?" I asked.

Domnall's expression tightened, but he said, "Callum is still under guard. He is well, I assure you."

"I'd like to see that for myself," I said.

Josh glared across the table, but I wouldn't back down on this. I'd barely thought about Callum since finding my mama. All of my thoughts had been consumed with worrying about her, and I felt guilty for not checking in on Callum since we'd left him in that room three days ago. I hated to think of him sitting alone, with the barest slit of a window to see outside.

Domnall wiped his mouth with a gray cloth napkin. "I do not think you are in any situation to make demands. You are a stranger here, and in case you had not yet noticed, I make the rules on this island."

"Where I come from, people are free to do what they want," I said.

Domnall's eyes flashed. "And where exactly is it you come from?"

Josh cleared his throat. "We are concerned about Callum. He has been a good friend to us, and he helped us find our way here. We want to know that he really is okay."

"Callum is being tended to as is the custom of our laws toward criminals," Domnall said. "He is currently awaiting judgment for this latest offense of breaking his banishment."

"He only did that for us," I said. "He never wanted to come here."

Domnall's mouth tightened into a thin line. "And he very well should have kept to that desire. He was found guilty of treason and murder, he is lucky he was not put to death five years ago. But we finfolk do not kill our own. He was given the harshest sentence we could—banishment from our island. He is the one who chose to break that sentence, and now he will face the consequences."

"So what are you going to do?" I asked. "Keep him locked away for the rest of his life?"

"I have not decided my judgment yet," Domnall said. He pushed his food around on his plate, frowning toward the table. "Perhaps I might be persuaded to go lightly on him..."

Josh raised an eyebrow. "How?"

Domnall stared at me, the lines in his face deepening. "Tell me where you come from and I will release your friend."

"Let me see Callum." I gripped the ornate silver fork in my fist to keep myself from trembling. I had no intention of telling Domnall anything, but I knew I had to play his game. Josh and I held a bargaining chip, and we needed to keep that power for as long as possible.

Domnall's gaze didn't flicker from mine for a long moment. Finally he nodded. "Very well, you may see him."

* * *

"Callum?"

He lay on the mattress, a blanket tangled around his legs. He still didn't have a prosthetic, to keep him from trying to escape, I guessed. At the sound of my voice, Callum lifted his head and half-turned toward the doorway where I stood. His eyes were hollow, dark circles lining both of them. He looked thinner and paler. Even his red hair looked duller than it had before.

I rushed across the room, kneeling next to him. "Are you okay?" I asked. I felt Josh's presence over my shoulder and heard his sharp intake of breath when he saw Callum.

"I'm fine." Callum's voice was raspy. He licked his dry lips. "What are you doing here?"

"We came to see if you're all right," Josh said. "Sailor demanded Domnall let us see you."

Callum raised his eyebrows. "And he actually agreed?"

"Not by choice. But he wants information from us, and he hopes I might give it to him if he lets us see you."

Callum's face darkened. "He wants to know where you came from, doesn't he?"

I nodded. "He keeps asking that I tell him where our people are. Why does he want them so badly?"

"He's delusional," Callum said. He laid his head back on the mattress and closed his eyes, as if the conversation had exhausted him.

I glared over my shoulder at the guard in the doorway. It wasn't Artair, but it was one of the guards who had been there when Josh and I were locked in the room too. "Has he had any water lately?" I asked.

"He is brought food and water three times a day," the guard told me, scowling. "It is his own fault that he does not eat."

My head whipped back toward Callum. "Why aren't you eating?"

Callum croaked a laugh. "Why should I? To extend my solitude in this room? I'd rather die quickly, if you don't mind."

I wanted to grab him by the shoulders and shake him hard. "You're not going to die," I said through clenched teeth.

He cracked one eye open and looked at me. "You may be able to order Domnall around, but you can't do the same to me."

I huffed an exasperated sigh, then pushed myself to my feet. I marched toward the guard, my hands on my hips. "Bring me a cup of water," I said.

The guard looked back at his companion who stood in the hall. Neither of them said a word.

"Now!" I shouted. "Saltwater. As salty as you can make it."

I thought I might have to throw an epic Sailor Mooring tantrum to get them to listen, but finally the guard in the hall disappeared. He returned a moment later, carrying a metal cup filled with water. Artair arrived at his heels, his face stern as he surveyed the room.

I took the cup and then went back to the mattress. Josh sat on Callum's other side and he helped me get Callum into a sitting position. I pressed the cup to Callum's lips, but he wouldn't open them.

"Drink," I ordered.

Callum didn't move.

"You should not waste your time on him," Artair said from behind me. His heavy footsteps thudded across the floor as he drew close. "If he wants to die, let him. He is condemned anyway."

I gritted my teeth, but didn't look at him. "Go away."

Artair didn't move. I felt him watching me as I pressed the cup harder against Callum's lips. "Drink," I said again.

"He is a murderer," Artair said. "He has turned against the teachings of his people. He has no right to live."

"Leave us alone," Josh said, his voice low and growling. "If you want to be in here, offer some help. Otherwise, you can go."

"He is not worth your concern," Artair said.

Callum opened his eyes and looked back at me. They were a dark green, so void of the life and sparkle they'd had back in Westray. He didn't look like himself at all. I pushed a lock of red curls off his forehead, surprised at how cold his skin was. I hated that we'd left him here to end up like this.

I leaned forward until my lips were next to his ear. Artair still hovered over us and I didn't want him to hear me. These words were for Callum alone.

"You helped me, now I'm going to help you," I whispered. "If you don't drink, I'll pour the whole damn glass over your head. I'll personally carry you outside and hold you under the water until you drink every last drop from the Atlantic Ocean."

When I pulled back, Callum had cracked a smile. "Is that a promise?" he asked.

"Drink." I put the cup to his lips again and this time he did drink, gulping down every drop of the water until the cup was empty. Josh eased him back down to the mattress and Callum sighed, panting heavily.

"You have seen him," Artair said. "You should leave now."

I wanted to scream at him for his unconcerned tone, but I knew it wouldn't do any good. If anything, it might put Callum into even more danger here in this place. I needed Domnall's kindness in order to save Callum from starving himself.

"Promise me you'll eat and drink," I said. "I don't want to find you like this again."

Callum looked slightly better already, but still

ghastly pale. My hair fell over my shoulders and he reached up to twist a lock of it around his finger.

"Does that mean you're coming back?" he asked.

I nodded. "Tomorrow. I'll come back tomorrow."

He smiled. "Then I'll eat. And drink. Because you asked me to."

I stayed like that, leaning over him, my hair twisted in his fingers. Something tickled across my scalp, a feeling I couldn't explain or identify. I had to resist the urge to place my hand against his cheek, brushing back his hair as I had before.

"Sailor," Josh said, placing a hand on my shoulder. "We should go."

I nodded, pulling back reluctantly. When Callum's hand fell away from my hair, an ache filled me as if something were missing.

Chapter 21

My only real glimpse of the finfolk village had been during our arrival and march through town as prisoners. It had looked strange and frightening, all of the unknown people staring at us.

Now as Josh and I walked toward the village square, I could see it was small, much smaller than I had originally thought. A few of the homes and shops looked abandoned, their windows and doors boarded up and sagging roofs hanging over them. Others had already half-crumbled into the water, while the ones that still stood were old and decaying.

It took every bit of willpower I had to not run straight back to the palace as we stepped into the village square, which was an open expanse of beach circled by homes and small shops. It was a warm, sunny day unlike the gray days before it, one of those days that begged to be enjoyed outside. A gentle breeze drifted in from the ocean and birds circled overhead. The sunny day had brought the people out of their homes. Some looked as if they had been swimming, their hair still dripping and leaving wet paths down their robes. Merchants had set up tents in the center of town and had wagons full of various fish and produce. Others sold jewelry made from seashells and sea glass.

I spotted Artair within the crowd and my stomach clenched. I scanned the area around him to see if Domnall was there too, but Artair stood with a woman and a small girl. His face had lost its usual frown and instead he looked relaxed. The little girl lifted her arms to him and Artair scooped her up, tickling her sides as he did.

I clenched my teeth together and turned away from the scene. Following Josh further into the market, I forced myself not to look back at Artair and what I assumed to be his family.

At first, the looks were only quick glances. Some people watched out of the corner of their eyes, while others glanced at us and then quickly away. But then I felt the gazes on my back, staring hard as I passed. When I looked over my shoulder, I found groups of people watching us, their expressions tense.

Josh stopped at a cart displaying seashell jewelry. "Doesn't this look like something Mara's dad would make?" he asked, pointing to an intricate bracelet.

I glanced at the bracelet, then scanned the watching crowd again. I couldn't tell whether Josh hadn't noticed the stares or if he had chosen to ignore them.

"Um," I said softly. "Maybe we should go back to the palace."

"How much is this?" Josh asked the merchant, ignoring me.

The man was old, his skin brown and weathered. His clear blue eyes flickered between the two of us for a long moment. Then he said, "It is not for sale."

Josh frowned. "But I thought—"

"You don't have any money anyway," I snapped. "Come on. We're wasting our time."

"For trade," the merchant said. "We trade here."

Josh nodded. "That makes sense. What do you trade for?"

The man leaned forward, his eyes wide. "I want a story," he whispered. "About the lost ones."

"A story?" I asked.

"We know you are not from near here," he said. "We want to know where the others are."

A sickening feeling settled into my stomach. Did Domnall have spies all over this village, all hoping to get the same information out of us?

I grabbed Josh's arm. "Come on," I ordered.

"No!" The merchant reached a hand toward me, but let it drop when I stepped back. "I did not mean..." He shook his head. "I am sorry. I should not ask these things."

He picked up the bracelet and offered it toward

Josh. "Take it."

Josh shook his head. "I can't—"

"Take it," the man urged.

His gaze flickered to a point over my shoulder and then his expression changed into something fierce. He hurled the bracelet at Josh, hitting him in the chest. "Take it and get out of here! I have no business with the likes of you."

The man's change in behavior seemed strange, until I turned and found Artair standing behind us. He was alone and no longer smiling and relaxed like he had been moments ago. Now he scowled down at us, his spear gripped tight in his left hand. The guard's stiff demeanor would make me angry too.

"Why are you not at the palace?" Artair asked.

I crossed my arms. "Are we supposed to stay there all day?"

"Domnall has seen that you have everything you need," Artair said. "You should not be here, bothering our citizens."

"We're not bothering anyone," Josh told him. "We're exploring the village, trying to get to know the people here."

Artair's eyes flashed at this. "And what exactly is it you hope to learn?"

"What are you afraid we might find?" I challenged.

Artair didn't say anything for a moment, then he held his shoulders back and stood straighter. "You should return to your suite before you make a nuisance of yourself. We are a peaceful people, and we do not take kindly to interruptions in our daily routines."

I snorted and rolled my eyes. "Yes, I've seen how peaceful you all are."

Artair scowled and he lowered his spear slightly in my direction, an unspoken threat. "It is my job to protect the people of this island," he said. "I will see to it that my job is carried out, in any way necessary. Now, I will ask you one last time to return to your suite."

My hands curled into fists and I glared up at Artair. But Josh put a hand on my shoulder to hold me back. "We're going," he said.

Chapter 22

"What are you doing here?" I wrinkled my nose at Domnall, who stood on the beach near the waiting boat. I had asked Artair earlier that day if he could take me to the peninsula again, but I hadn't been prepared for Domnall's presence. It was bad enough seeing Artair after our encounter at the village square the day before.

"I thought I would join you today." Domnall gave me his charming smile, which only made my stomach twist in nervousness. Whenever I was at the palace, I stayed in our suite as much as possible. I could feel Domnall watching me whenever I roamed around the halls or the grounds. He was always in the shadows or looking down at me from a balcony or window. He rarely spoke, just watched. If it wasn't for Callum still being locked away in the palace, I would have left long ago.

Josh helped me into the boat, both of us ignoring Domnall's outstretched arm. We had talked about Domnall's watching me, and neither of us felt comfortable with him.

The boat rocked slightly as Artair rowed out into the bay. I kept my gaze focused on the crumbling homes that dotted the peninsula ahead of us, though I felt Domnall's presence behind me. I knew if I looked over my shoulder, I'd find his blue eyes locked on me.

The boat slid into place next to the dock, and I climbed out as soon as it had stopped, not waiting for Artair to tie it off.

"I want to go in alone," I said.

"But—" Josh started.

I shook my head, cutting him off. "It might be easier for her if only person is there at a time." I knew Josh was getting impatient to ask his questions. But what would be the point? She wouldn't remember anything anyway.

Josh and Domnall followed me toward the village. When I reached the door with the lily carved into it, I took a deep breath and then stepped through, knocking softly as I entered.

Mama sat at her desk again in front of the window, only this time she wasn't bent over the papers in front of her. She sat straight in her wooden chair, her hands clasped together in her lap and her face turned toward the window. Through the glass, she had a great view of the ocean. White-capped waves rippled across the surface far offshore and birds dove and arced through the air above the water. The ever present mists rolled toward the horizon.

"Mama?" I knelt next to her, putting a hand gently on hers. The warmth and solidness of her body gave me comfort. She was thin, and the skin of her face hung loose and dull. But she was here and not an image created by the finfolk song. If I looked closely, I could see her resemblance to Grandma. They had the same wide blue eyes and curving nose.

She didn't look away from the window, but she spoke. "I think I'll go swimming today," she said. "I haven't been in a long time."

I couldn't tell if she knew where she was. Or even what day it was.

"Maybe down by the pier," she went on. "I always like jumping off the end." She laughed. "Sometimes I do it when the tourists are fishing. It always startles them."

My shoulders slumped. She was obviously still confused. The pier she spoke of was probably the Swans Landing Pier, which had been broken during a hurricane ten years ago and never repaired. No one fished there anymore, not that many tourists even came to our island at all these days. Not like they used to, in Grandma's stories about the old days, before my father died and before everything changed.

"Mama, it's me," I said gently. "It's Sailor. We're not in Swans Landing, we're in Hether Blether. Do you remember coming here?"

She turned her head toward me, blinking slowly as if trying to focus on my face. "Sailor?" she asked, her brow wrinkling. "That's a pretty name."

I smirked. "You should think so, you gave it to me."

Mama suddenly sat up, shuffling the papers on her desk into a messy stack. "I forgot I have to work at the store today. Daddy is expecting me."

She stood and walked across the room to an old wardrobe, pulling open the door and pushing through the couple of robes that hung inside. They were old and shapeless, much like the brown one she wore.

"Mama," I said. "It's okay. You're not working today."

But she didn't listen as she searched through the clothes again. "I promised Daddy I would work there this summer," she said. "He was so happy when I said I would."

It was strange to hear her speak of her father. I knew Jim Moody was my granddaddy and I knew he loved Grandma. But he had never spoken of my mother to me and Grandma never mentioned him except when she talked about the variety store he owned and where she worked sometimes. Jim—I had never been able to call him Granddaddy—rarely ever spoke to me.

Mama seemed to have already lost this train of thought and she returned to her desk, sitting down and sorting through her papers. They were drawings, mostly of the ocean or trees or birds. I stood next to her and gently touched her shoulder as she shuffled through each sheet. She didn't flinch or move away at my touch, so I left my hand there to feel some kind of connection to her, even if she didn't know who I was.

When she moved one paper to the back of the stack, the drawing on top made me gasp. It was the narrow strip of beach at Pirate's Cove, back in Swans Landing. The beach was accessed by a narrow path that wound through the forest of live oak trees on the southern end of the island. It was small and mostly overlooked by anyone who didn't know Swans Landing well. It was the only place where finfolk could swim without being seen by anyone else.

"You remember," I said to my mother. I pointed to the picture. "You know this place."

"Pirate's Cove," she said. She stared down at the drawing in her hand, her mouth turned into a frown. "I used to go swimming with him there. It was our special spot."

My heart pounded against my ribs. My knees threatened to buckle and give out. I eased myself down until I squatted next to her. Did I dare ask her the question on my tongue? I didn't want to push her, but I had to make some progress.

"Mama, do you remember what happened to Oliver Canavan?" I asked.

"He..." Mama's mouth trembled. "I didn't mean...He shouldn't have been there."

"What happened?" I asked gently. "Please, Mama, it's important. Can you remember what happened the night Oliver died?"

Mama's eyes turned toward me. They were wide and her face was pale. "Oliver is...dead?" she asked in a small voice.

"Mama—"

But already her eyes had taken on the vacant look. She shook her head, whipping her hair back and forth. "No. No, no, no!"

At her shout, the door burst open and Josh ran into the room. He skidded to a stop, staring down at my mother. She still sat in the chair at the desk, but now she was shaking violently and screaming "No!" over and over.

"Mama!" I said, trying to reach for her. She shrieked and backed away from my grasp, knocking the chair over as she stumbled to her feet. She backed into the corner, still shaking and screaming.

"Sailor, don't," Josh said when I started toward her. He looked at Mama, his lips pressed into a tight, white line. "Ms. Mooring?"

Mama's mouth opened, but no sound came out. Her face paled, then she broke into a wide smile. "Oliver," she said, reaching toward Josh. "I found it, like you said."

Josh swallowed hard. "Ms. Mooring, my name is Josh Canavan. I'm Oliver's son."

Confusion flitted across Mama's face. "Oliver?" she asked.

"He died," Josh said softly. "A long time ago."

Mama crumpled to the floor, pressing her hands against her face. She let out a wail of, "No! No! No!"

I knelt next to her, but Mama batted at me wildly, scratching my arms with her ragged nails.

"We should leave," Josh said, pulling me to my feet.

"But she's needs help," I said.

Josh shook his head. "We can't help her right now."

I let him lead me out of the room. I grabbed the drawing of Pirate's Cove off the desk and folded it quickly until it was small enough to hide in my fist.

Domnall waited for us outside the hut, looking unconcerned even though we could still hear Mama's shouting.

"Do you understand yet what the human world does to finfolk?" Domnall asked, his gaze locked on me.

I walked past him without answering.

"There is a reason we choose banishment for those who commit the unpardonable crimes," Domnall went on. I heard the crunch of his footsteps on the sandy ground behind me. "The human world kills us, slowly or quickly, it does not matter. It always ends like this. Your mother is proof of this. You see what she is now. That is what the taint of humans has done to her. It is what they will do to us here in Hether Blether, unless we can stop it."

I spun around to face him. "What about me?" I asked. "What about Josh? We're not like that. Callum isn't like that. What does that mean to your theory about the human taint?"

Domnall stared evenly at me, despite my outburst. "Callum has only been in the human world for five years. You and your brother are also fairly young.

172

Perhaps you have not yet succumbed to the destruction that world is doing to you."

"Humans didn't do this," Josh said. "Something else happened to make her like that. Maybe something you did, for all we know."

"She was found in that condition sixteen years ago," Domnall said. "I have had my best people of medicine tend to her, yet nothing has changed. She is not the only one. There are records of others, in the palace archives. Another like your mother arrived years ago when I was a young boy. This woman had come from your world and found her way to ours. She also was disturbed, as your mother is. The human world is not the place for our kind. We have to stop their spread from reaching Hether Blether."

I squeezed my fist where I had hidden Mama's drawing. "I'm not helping you find and destroy my home."

Domnall laughed. "I do not want to destroy it, I assure you. I only want to protect our people before they become ill."

"No one is sick!" I shouted.

"Have you never known anyone else who behaves the way your mother does?" Domnall asked.

I stopped and turned to face him. My gaze met Josh's over Domnall's shoulder. We both knew someone else who behaved like that—Josh's mother.

But Domnall's reasoning still didn't make sense. Mrs. Canavan wasn't finfolk. She was human, and she hated the finfolk. She would have been happy to see all of us leave Swans Landing.

Domnall looked between us, his face grave. "It is not only your people who are at risk. Hether Blether itself is dying."

Josh and I turned toward Domnall. "What?" Josh asked.

"What do you mean?" I asked.

Domnall's expression was unchanged. "I mean exactly what I said. Without the protection that has divided us from the human world for countless centuries, Hether Blether will cease to exist as we know it. The infection that has affected your mother's mind will spread to the finfolk here, as well as the ones in your world. The finfolk race is dying out. And if we do nothing, our kind will not survive."

He stepped forward, holding his hands out toward me, palms up. "I come to you not as a king, but as a man asking for your help."

"We're not doctors. We have no special magic to put the protection back in place."

"You are wrong," Domnall said. "Every finfolk who sings the song can put the protection back and chase away the taint in this land. It is a song of rebirth, and it can be used to make us new and remake Hether Blether. You can help by telling me where the others like you are. If we can bring them back, we can save Hether Blether and all of the finfolk people." He stepped back, dropping his hands, his expression solemn. "The choice is yours."

Chapter 23

Callum stood near the slit of a window, balancing himself on his leg, when I entered his room.

"Feeling better?" I asked. He certainly looked better. Color had returned to his face and he was gaining back some weight already.

"I'd be better if I could breathe in the salt air through more than this tiny window," he said. "Finfolk aren't meant to be kept away from the sea, even ones who aren't really finfolk anymore."

Once a finfolk knows the salt water, it's impossible for him or her to leave it for long.

"Why can't you change?" I asked as I sat down on the corner of the mattress, wrapping my arms around myself. I was grateful for the chance to think about something other than my mother.

Callum hesitated, then worked his way toward the mattress, steadying himself against the wall as he hopped.

"Part of my punishment was that I would lose the ability to swim like I once had," he said. He gestured toward his leg. "This apparently wasn't enough for Domnall. He had to take away all chances of my return."

I gulped at the realization that Domnall had cut off Callum's leg. "But how? How is it possible to make you not finfolk?"

"I am still finfolk. What I said before about not being finfolk is not technically true. I can still sing and I need to be near the ocean to survive. But I can no longer change form. Not that changing would do me much good, considering I would be incomplete without my leg. But as to how it is possible, it is done with a song."

I raised my eyebrows, remembering the finfolk healing the woman on the beach. "You mean by combining the songs of earth and water into one?"

Now Callum looked surprised. "How do you know about that? I did not think your people had retained much of the ancient knowledge."

"We didn't," I said. "At least, I've never heard of anyone doing it back home. But I saw some people heal a woman on the beach a few days ago."

"It is an old power," Callum said. "The song the finfolk on the beach sang is one version of it, a simpler one. The one that was used on me is much older and more complex. Like how the healing song can be used to heal wounds while changing forms, this song can be used to keep someone locked in one form." He shook his head. "I can't say precisely how it works, but it blocks the body's ability to shift."

"That's impossible," I said.

He smirked. "You saw the evidence for yourself. I swam for hours with you and Josh, yet I never changed. I'm stuck in my human form."

"Can it be reversed? Could someone sing the song again and let you change?"

"Maybe," Callum said. "It has never been done that I know of. The song is usually done only on finfolk who have committed a big enough sin to be stripped of their rights. Once they are banished from Hether Blether, they never come back."

"Except you," I said.

Callum grinned. "Aye, well, I had the foresight to steal the key before I left." He winked.

I tried to laugh, but the thought of Callum being stuck in one form forever was overwhelming. I couldn't imagine not swimming as a finfolk. "It's not right," I said. "Domnall shouldn't have done that to you."

"It is only done in certain circumstances. We don't believe in killing our own kind, since each finfolk carries a part of our people's essence. Killing each other would make all of us weaker. But we can take away the ability to change in place of death. It is a death of its own kind."

I thought about my mother, trapped here on this island for sixteen years. Had Domnall done this to her, like he had to Callum? Had she ever tried to go back home?

"I'm sorry," Callum said, seeing my frown. "I didn't mean to upset you with this."

I shook my head. "No, it's not that." I swallowed, trying to figure out the best way to explain everything that had happened that day. I hadn't told him yet about my mama. I hadn't been able to talk much about her.

"I found my mother," I finally said.

"Here in Hether Blether?" he asked.

"On the peninsula."

"Your mother is there? You're sure of that?"

I nodded. "I've visited her a few times. I went today. She's not...healthy."

"How long has she been here?"

"Sixteen years. She somehow found her way here."

Callum's eyes widened. "There have been rumors before, of people from outside our island finding their way here. But I always thought it was just that, rumors. How could she have been here that long and no one knew?"

"Domnall knew." I dug my fingernails into the palms of my hands. "I don't know what to believe. He says she's been like that since she got here, but I can't help wondering if he did something to her. She doesn't seem to know where she is or even when it is. She won't respond to me, even when I tell her who I am. She wasn't like that when she left our home. Grandma would have told me if my mama had been like that."

Callum placed a hand over mine. His hands were so much larger than mine, though his skin was much paler and freckles dotted the back of his hand. "Perhaps," he said. "Or perhaps your grandmother wanted to protect you from the truth."

"She's not crazy!" I shouted at him. "Something happened. Either something here or something back home. Something made her like this."

"Then you have to try to find out what exactly it was," Callum said. "Keep talking to her."

"Domnall said my mother's condition is caused by an infection from living in the human world. He says this taint or whatever it is is spreading to Hether Blether, and he needs to bring the lost finfolk back home in order to save the island."

Callum sighed. "Domnall has a lot of ideas lately."

"What do you think?" I asked.

He looked at me, his expression grave. "I think you should leave Hether Blether as soon as possible and never come back."

I swallowed at the tone in his words. "Why?"

"Because this land is not healthy," Callum said. "Domnall is not healthy. He doesn't know you're part human, but once he finds out he will do whatever he thinks is best to get rid of the tainted part of you and your people. The song can be used in other ways, Sailor. He can block the part of you that makes you human if he figures out how to change the song."

"So Josh and I are in danger?" I asked.

"I think so, yes. Take your brother and go. Swim toward the mists for as long as you can. Eventually you'll find your way through to the human world."

"What about you?" I asked.

Callum shrugged. "I'm a deformed finfolk. Don't concern yourself about me."

I was aware of the guards outside the door, so I kept my voice low. "But you're the reason we even made it here. I can't leave you behind to rot away in this room."

"You can't save me," Callum said. "I'm not important, nothing to worry about."

Tears stung my eyes suddenly. "You're important to me," I said.

Time froze as my words hung in the air. The muscles along Callum's neck twitched as he swallowed. His hand was still clasped over mine, his fingers squeezing tight.

A heartbeat passed, then another.

And then my lips met his. I didn't know who had leaned forward, maybe both of us did, but my mouth pressed to his, crushing lips in a kiss that sent static tingling through my body. His hands moved into my hair, grasping my head and pressing me closer to him. I wrapped my arms around his shoulders, feeling the width and strength and solidity of his body.

When we were eleven, Dylan and I had kissed once. I had wanted to have my first kiss and in my mind, it would always be Dylan and me. We were meant for each other from the moment we were born. Everything that had ever happened in my life had happened with Dylan at my side. So we had kissed, the only time Dylan had ever kissed me, despite my numerous attempts to make him see that I had always been the one meant for him.

But this...no one had ever kissed me like this.

I wrenched myself away from Callum, stumbling as I pushed myself up from the mattress. His lips were red and he seemed as breathless as I felt. He blinked, his eyes showing a dazed look.

"I—I'm sorry," I blurted out. "I have to go."

"Sailor—"

I pulled open the wooden door and then tore down the hall, past the stunned guards.

Chapter 24

"Leaving so soon?"

Domnall stepped out of the shadows at the end of the hallway, stopping my run toward the stairs. His blue eyes looked me over. "You are flushed," he said. "Are you unwell?"

"I'm fine," I said quickly. I tried to calm my panting breaths, but my heart still thudded against my chest and my pulse pounded in my ears.

"Perhaps you would like to sit down?" Without waiting for my response, Domnall gripped my elbow and led me down the stairs. He took me to the place where he had first offered to take me to my mother. The door in the floor was open and water rippled below. A door to my left showed a bedroom decorated in matching dark blue and gray. My gaze found the sightless statues watching me from the corners and I looked away quickly, not wanting to think about the humans that might have lost their lives when the ships carrying them sank.

My tongue scratched against the roof of my dry mouth. "I should go back to my room," I said.

Domnall closed the door and then crossed the room to a table where a silver pitcher and cups sat. He poured a cup of water and then offered it to me.

"Drink," he said. "You look disturbed. If Callum did anything to harm you—"

"He didn't harm me!" I said.

Domnall blinked once, his expression neutral. He offered the cup again and this time I took it, clutching it tightly to keep my hands from shaking.

"You have been spending a lot of time with Callum lately."

"He's stuck in a room by himself. He needs company."

"Aye," Domnall said. He walked around me in a slow circle. "But I notice your brother only comes occasionally, while you are there often, sitting alone in that room with him. It makes one wonder..."

I glared at Domnall's head as he continued around me. "Wonder what?"

"One wonders what exactly is the nature of your relationship with Callum?" Now Domnall stopped in front of me, gazing back at me intently.

"There is no relationship between us," I said, clenching my teeth together. "I am keeping him company because you feel the need to keep him locked away."

Domnall shrugged. "It is what we always do with prisoners who are awaiting judgment."

"So judge him already!" My voice echoed off the sandy walls around us. "Are you keeping him locked up like that to torment him?"

Something flickered at the corners of Domnall's mouth, a smile maybe, or a grimace. It was gone so quickly I couldn't be sure. "Has Callum told you what he did to cause his banishment?"

"No," I said, sighing. "And neither have you, for that matter."

Domnall stopped next to a table, pulling open a drawer and staring down into it for a moment. From my position I couldn't see what held his interest.

"I am only the judge, as necessitated by my role here," Domnall said. "Callum must atone for his sins."

"He said he didn't do it. What evidence do you have to keep him?"

Domnall's eyes were dark, his forehead creased into a deep scowl. "I have his own confession."

My blood turned cold in my veins. But Callum had told me he hadn't killed anyone. If he had confessed, why did he now deny it? Who was telling the truth around here?

My legs trembled and I leaned back to brace myself against the wall. Callum's kiss still tingled on my lips. How could he kill someone, and yet sit on that bed looking so vulnerable and innocent? Had he played with my emotions to get me on his side?

"You know he is a criminal. You have seen it." He reached into the open drawer and retrieved a twisted piece of metal. The key that had led us to Hether Blether. "He stole this when he was banished from our island. He took it because he always intended to break his punishment someday."

Anger and confusion battled inside me. I didn't know who I should trust.

"Yet," Domnall went on, returning the key to the drawer, "that is a smaller crime. As to the other crimes, perhaps he was under emotional duress at the time of his confession. Sometimes the mind does not always portray things accurately, correct? For instance, looking at the emotions flitting across your face, one might think you had an interest in Callum. Some feelings toward him, perhaps. But one might be wrong, might they not?"

"I have no interest in Callum," I said, the words almost choking me.

Domnall clasped his hands together behind his back. "Good. Because I am close to my judgment of him, and there are those who urge me to cut off his other leg so he might never be able to swim again."

I gasped. "You can't do that!"

Domnall blinked. "I thought you did not care for him."

"Not caring for him doesn't mean I think you should amputate his leg!"

"Then perhaps we can make a deal." Domnall's voice was solemn, his gaze burning into me.

"What kind of a deal?" I asked, narrowing my eyes.

"I could be convinced to release Callum," Domnall said. "Into your care."

"Why would you do that?"

"Callum has already atoned for his earlier crimes. Breaking banishment is much more innocent than murder and treason. I could be convinced to overlook this incident and let Callum remain under your supervision during your stay here."

Domnall's words swirled in my head for a moment. "During our stay?" I asked. "Does that mean you're letting us leave the island? When we want?"

He held his hands out to me, palms up. "I am not a tyrant, Sailor. I am merely trying to protect and lead my people into a brighter future. I will not stop those who wish to leave our shores. I only ask for the chance to bring back those who are lost, those who wish to return home."

His words sounded rational. There were others in Swans Landing who had mentioned wanting to go back to our ancestral home. Not everyone was happy among the humans. Shouldn't they have the chance to come to Hether Blether if they wanted it?

"The finfolk who don't want to come here, you'll leave them alone?" I asked.

Domnall's smile spread and he didn't look away from me as he said, "You have my word that anyone who wishes to stay behind will have that opportunity." He stepped forward and reached for my hand, squeezing it tight in his. "You have the chance to save both Callum and this island. We will forever be indebted to you. Think about it, Sailor. You could have anything you want in return. Money, power." He stepped toward me, reaching up to brush his fingers over my cheek. "A family. Is that not what you came all this way to find?"

I swallowed, taking a deep breath as I thought over my options. I could leave Callum to spend the rest of his life without legs, or I could free him. I could keep Swans Landing hidden from Domnall and let Hether Blether die, or I could help the finfolk race secure their future. I could live happily in Hether Blether with Mama, far away from the humans who hated me and memories of a life I was robbed of living. Maybe I could even convince Grandma to come here too, once she heard Mama was here.

What had Swans Landing ever given me?

I let out a long breath. There was really only one option.

* * *

Josh stood quickly when I entered the suite with Callum at my heels. His eyes widened as he looked between the two of us. "How?" was all he said.

"Domnall agreed to let Callum go," I said.

The sun was beginning to set over the western sky. Through the window, I could see the clouds and mist turning red-gold. I had refused to leave Callum's room until he could walk out with me. It had taken a couple of hours for the woodcarver to create and fit Callum with a new prosthetic. It was cruder than the one he'd had before; apparently, finfolk medicine wasn't as advanced as the human world. But he could stand again and walk, and it filled me with pride that I could help him.

Though Callum didn't exactly look appreciative of that help. I glanced his away, but still, his face was twisted into a scowl.

"She shouldn't have freed me," Callum said. He walked across the room and sat down at the table where Josh had been sitting before we'd entered. He stretched his prosthetic before him, rubbing the place where the wooden leg was secured to his flesh.

"Sorry," I snapped, crossing my arms. "I didn't know you wanted to stay locked up forever. I'm sure Domnall will let you go back to your room."

Callum scowled through the hair that had fallen in front of his eyes as he leaned over. "Domnall doesn't do favors. You had to give him something he wanted in return."

Josh's gaze snapped to me. "What did he want, Sailor?"

"He wanted to know where Swans Landing is," I said.

Josh gasped, his face paling of all color. "I can't believe you did that." He stomped across the floor toward me. "You've put everyone in danger, do you realize that? Do you ever even stop and think before you do things? Do you think about anyone other than yourself?"

"I do think about something other than myself!" Tears blurred my vision, but I would not let them fall. I squeezed my fists at my sides, my jaw tight. "If I didn't give Domnall what he wanted, he was going to sentence Callum for breaking his banishment."

"I've been sentenced before," Callum told me. "I can deal with Domnall."

"He was going to cut off your leg," I said. "He would make sure you couldn't ever swim back to Hether Blether. Make it so you couldn't swim at all."

Silence hung in the room after my words. Josh's face had paled and he looked ashamed. Good. I hoped he was ashamed of what he'd said about me.

Callum's scowl had disappeared. He swallowed, opened and closed his mouth, then opened it again and finally spoke. "Thank you," he said, "for what you did. But you didn't have to sacrifice your home for me. I can't live with the knowledge that my freedom comes at the price of your people. My life isn't worth theirs."

189

My chin quivered slightly, but I gritted my teeth harder and crossed my arms tight over my chest. "Yeah, well, you're welcome anyway."

I stomped to my room, slamming the door behind me. It shouldn't have upset me, the way everyone automatically assumed the worst about me. I should have been used to it.

I scrubbed my eyes at the sound of the knock on the door. It creaked open slightly and Josh stuck his head in.

"Can I come in?" he asked.

I shrugged, keeping my gaze locked on the shells embedded into the wall near my bed.

I heard him shuffle across the floor and then his weight caused me to shift a little on the mattress.

"I'm sorry," he said. "I shouldn't have said those things."

"Yes, you should," I said. "I'm a screw up. My entire existence is a mistake that should never have happened."

"That's not true," Josh stated. "You're my sister. And I know you being here means my dad had an affair, but I don't blame you. It doesn't affect how I see you."

I snorted. "You're the only one who thinks that way then."

"No, I'm not," Josh said. "Miss Gale thinks that way. So does Dylan."

I closed my eyes, thinking about Grandma and

Dylan, four thousand miles away on the other side of the ocean. I missed them so much. It had been too long since I'd seen them.

"I wish I could open my eyes and be home again," I said.

"Me too," Josh said softly.

But when I opened my eyes, we still sat in my room in the palace in Hether Blether.

It was just as well. If I went back to Swans Landing, I'd still be in the same situation I'd always been in. It would never change, never get better. Maybe Hether Blether was where our people belonged. Maybe Domnall could help us all.

"So," Josh said, "did you really tell Domnall how to find Swans Landing?"

"I had no choice," I said. "He wouldn't have let Callum go if I didn't."

Josh frowned. "What does he plan to do once he gets there?"

I shrugged. "He wants to talk to the finfolk and ask them to come back to Hether Blether. That's not such a bad thing. I'm sure there may be some who would like to come here."

Josh closed his eyes and shook his head. "It's not just us or the finfolk back home we have to worry about, Sailor."

"He promised he wouldn't hurt anyone," I said.

"But what did he say about the humans?" asked another voice.

Josh and I looked toward the door, where Callum leaned against the frame.

"What?" I asked.

"What did Domnall say he would do to the humans he found?" Callum asked in a quiet voice.

"Nothing. He didn't say anything about the humans."

"Did you get his vow that he wouldn't harm them?"

Something prickled along my scalp, a coldness racing down my spine. "No, I didn't ask about the humans."

Callum looked grave. "Remember I told you not to let anyone here know you have human blood? Domnall blames humans for everything that has gone wrong in Hether Blether these last centuries. The only reason he doesn't go to Westray or anywhere else near here is because he knows he's outnumbered. But in your home, if there are finfolk already living there, perhaps he thinks he has a chance."

"A chance to do what?" Josh asked.

"A chance to rid finfolk of the human taint," Callum told him. "Domnall wants to take over human lands, take back what the humans once took from us."

"And what will he do to the humans?" I asked.

Callum gestured toward his leg. "Domnall couldn't kill me because killing a fellow finfolk is the greatest sin our kind can commit. But that doesn't mean he feels the same way about humans."

Josh's face was so white he looked as if he might

pass out. What would Domnall do if my directions led him toward a human city?

And if Domnall found out Josh and I had human blood, how worthy would he consider us?

Josh leaned forward, his fists clenched in his lap. "This isn't good. We have to do something."

"What can we do?" I asked.

I looked at both Callum and Josh, but neither of them looked as though they had any answers.

Chapter 25

Callum and I were quiet as we followed the path from the palace toward the village square. He had been desperate to get out of the palace and he sucked in deep breaths as he walked, lifting his face toward the hazy sun overhead.

I couldn't help watching him from the corner of my eye. I ducked my head a little so Callum couldn't see the flush that crept up my neck. We hadn't talked about what had happened between us, mostly because we hadn't had time alone. It was hard to get any privacy with Josh around. He had stayed behind to try to catch fish on the beach under our suite again. This walk was the first moment Callum and I had been alone since Domnall had freed him.

I cleared my throat once, but then I couldn't think of anything to say. The words I wanted to say wouldn't come out.

Callum took a deep breath, and I thought he might speak. My heartbeat quickened as I waited.

But he said nothing.

I cleared my throat again. "How is your leg?" I asked.

"It's fine," Callum said. "It will get me where I want to go." He limped noticeably, and the tight line of his mouth let me know the crudely carved prosthetic was not like the one he was used to.

"I'm sorry," I said. "For everything. It's all my fault."

He smirked. "Aye, it is."

I clamped my mouth shut, stung. He didn't have to sound so angry about it. I had apologized already. I'd gotten him out of his prison. Didn't that count for anything?

"But," Callum went on, "what has happened has happened, and neither of us can change it. So there is no reason to dwell on it, no reason to keep apologizing. I could have left Hether Blether that day on the beach. I could have stayed in the water or tried to swim back to Westray. It's as much my own doing that I ended up here as it is yours."

Birds chirped in the trees around us. The morning was still misty and gray, with a slight chill to the air. I wrapped my arms around myself for warmth.

"So are we going to talk about what happened?" I asked.

"I thought we were talking about what happened," he said, with a small smile.

My cheeks burned. "I mean, you know. The kiss."

"Ah." Callum shrugged. "I thought you were unable to resist my natural charms."

I scoffed. "I think you're the one with the problem. You practically threw yourself all over me."

"I am in perfect control of myself," Callum said. "You, on the other hand, have already shown that you act without thinking."

I scowled and then walked faster, leaving him behind. I didn't care that he struggled with the wooden prosthetic. Let him suffer while trying to catch up with me. I wasn't some sex-crazed girl who threw herself at pathetic guys.

"Sailor," Callum called behind me. "I was joking."

But I didn't slow down. I kept walking fast, and once we reached the village, I turned and headed straight for the market wagons. I refused to look back to see how far behind Callum was.

The sight of the colorful rhubarb and berries in one wagon made my stomach growl. I breathed in the sweet scent, thankful to smell something other than fish, though there was plenty of it too in another wagon.

I noticed a group of people in the center of the

square and walked closer to see what had their attention. A hand on my elbow stopped me.

"Stay back," Callum told me. "Don't draw attention to yourself."

"Why?" I asked.

But I spotted a familiar face through a break in the crowd that made my stomach twist. Artair, Domnall's guardsman, stood in the center of the group.

"We are asking for all healthy, able-bodied finfolk to accompany us on this journey," Artair said in a thundering voice. "It will not be easy, and you will be away from home for a long time. But it is our duty to find our lost brethren and to save them from the human world. Our survival depends on their survival. Bringing the lost ones home will make Hether Blether strong again. It will reopen the way to Finfolkaheem. We will ensure the survival of our race."

Cold sweat beaded along my skin as Artair's words sank into my head.

"Domnall isn't wasting any time," Callum said grimly.

"So he really intends to go out and look for the other finfolk," I said. A part of me had hoped Domnall would decide the trip was too dangerous to actually do and he'd never try it.

"He does," Callum said softly. "And that means your people are in more danger than you know. Either Domnall will actually find someone when he follows the directions you gave him, or else he'll find out you lied and he will not let you go unpunished."

I swallowed the lump in my throat. "So what should I do?"

Callum turned me around, still gripping my elbow tight. We hurried back across the square toward the path to the palace. "You need to go home. As soon as possible. Get out of here before Domnall begins his journey so he can't follow you. Go back to where you came from and warn your people about what may come. I don't think Domnall will give up until he finds what he wants."

I stopped, pulling my arm from his grasp. "What about you?" I asked.

"What about me?" Callum gestured toward his leg. "I'm not whole, Sailor. I can't even change forms anymore. I could never make the swim with you. Get your brother and go. Don't worry about me."

I dug my nails into my palms, trying to hold back tears that stung my eyes. "I'm not leaving you here. Not after what Domnall has already done to you."

"Sailor—"

But Callum was cut off by the approach of an older man with thin graying hair. A deep scowl was etched into the lines on his face.

"Murderer," he said. Then he spat at Callum's feet.

A woman passing by stopped to glare at Callum. "Traitor," she growled. "You are unfit to be called finfolk."

I stepped in front of Callum. "Leave him alone," I

said.

Callum put his hand on my shoulder. "It's fine, Sailor. Let them say what they want to say."

"No." I glared at the man and woman. "They can't treat you like this."

The two turned their angry glares toward me as other people passing by stopped to watch too. Soon there would be a crowd of angry finfolk around us.

"Let's go," Callum said. I let him pull me away from the square. The finfolk parted to allow us to pass, but when I glanced over my shoulder, they still stared after us.

"Are you all right?" Callum asked softly.

"What was that?"

Callum shook his head. "Just their own fear."

I pulled him to a stop in front of me. I looked up into his bright green eyes, refusing to break his gaze. "Callum, if you want me to help you and get out of here, you have to be honest with me. You have to tell me exactly what happened to cause your banishment."

Callum studied me for a long time. Finally, he nodded. "All right. Follow me."

* * *

We stood on a large dune, beyond the village. We had almost walked all the way back to where we had first arrived on the island. I wasn't sure how long ago that had been. Weeks, maybe a month?

Morning mist still hung over the ocean on this part of the beach. The cold wind whipped at my hair and the robe Domnall had provided me with. I looked like any other finfolk girl in Hether Blether. But my eyes scanned the hazy horizon far out at sea, looking for the place I knew I could never see from here.

Maybe it was time to go home, but I couldn't leave without Callum or my mama. Neither of them were in a condition to survive swimming that far.

"I used to come here to watch the sunset with my sister," Callum said.

His cheeks were rosy in the cold air. "Pearl?" I asked, remembering the name of the person he had once compared me to.

He nodded. "She was older than me by several years. Our parents died when I was seven. A virus hit Hether Blether back then and a lot of finfolk died. I almost died along with my parents, but Pearl nursed me back to health. Our grandparents, an aunt, two uncles, and a cousin all died as well. And so then, it was just the two of us. Pearl raised me."

"So what happened?" I asked. "What does this have to do with..." My voice trailed off as a thought hit me and I sucked in a sharp breath as a chill spread through me. "Did you...you murdered your sister?"

"*No.*" Callum's green eyes bored into mine. "No. She meant everything to me." His voice cracked and his chin quivered slightly.

"Then what?" I asked. "How did she die?"

"It was a mistake," Callum said, squeezing his eyes shut. "A stupid, terrible mistake. I was fourteen at the time, and I thought I knew everything. I thought I knew what was best for Hether Blether. The virus that killed my parents was only a symptom of something that had been happening to the island for a long time. *We don't get sick here,* Sailor. We don't die of disease, it doesn't happen." His shoulders slumped. "Or at least, that was the way it used to be. Now, with the protection around the island failing, we're being exposed to diseases we've never experienced before. But it doesn't have to be a death sentence. We can live in the human world, we can be a part of it and use their medicine to treat ourselves. That is what I was trying to do that day."

Callum took a deep breath. "But Pearl tried to talk me out of it. She worried that exposing our world to the humans would cause more trouble than it would help. I wanted to show everyone I wasn't some kid with crazy ideas. I swam for Westray. I didn't realize how rough the sea was that day. I grew tired quickly and couldn't find my way back to Hether Blether. When I didn't come home that night, Pearl went out looking for me. She found me, I don't know how, but she had some kind of instinct that led her to me.

"But we were close to the shores of Westray," Callum went on. "Close to the cliff, where the lighthouse is. It was so dark, we couldn't see anything except the light shining high above us. The water got rougher as we swam closer to the island. I tried to hold onto her. If we had been able to stick together, maybe our combined strength could have fought back against the current. We could have found our way around the cliffs to safer ground. But I lost my grip on her. I called for her, but she didn't answer. I stayed in that water all night, calling for her and searching."

His shoulders shuddered as he sucked in a deep breath. I squeezed his hand and stepped closer to him.

"What happened?" I asked gently.

"When the morning came, I was able to follow the cliff around the island toward lower ground. And then I saw Pearl, washed up on shore. I went to her, but she was already gone. She'd hit her head on the rocks along the cliff. She lay there, with her eyes wide open and staring up at the sky. I wanted to bring her back to Hether Blether, but then I heard someone coming down the beach toward us. I got scared. I didn't know what else to do, so I left her there and went back into the water."

I wrapped my arms around him, pressing my cheek against his shoulder. "What did they do with her body?" I asked. "Did they know she was finfolk?"

He shook his head. "I don't think so. Somehow her body had changed back to human form, so she had legs. I watched from the water as the man who found her called for help. They carried her off. After my banishment, when I returned to Westray, I found out from old newspapers that there had been news stories asking for information on her identity. But no one knew who she was, so eventually, she was buried in an unnamed grave.

"When I came back home and told everyone what had happened, Domnall convinced them that my actions were treason," Callum said. "I had risked exposing all of them. And since my actions led to the death of my sister, I was labeled a murderer."

"But it was an accident," I said. "You didn't kill her."

Callum shrugged. "Her death is my fault. So Domnall was right to banish me."

"And your leg?" I asked.

"It was the most severe punishment Domnall could give me. I can't swim as well as a whole finfolk can. Cutting off my leg and taking away my ability to change was supposed to keep me from coming back to Hether Blether." He smirked. "We see how well that worked out."

"But it's barbaric," I insisted. "You never intentionally set out to hurt anyone. Cutting off your leg for that is wrong."

He ran a hand through his hair. "It's what I deserve, Sailor. If I hadn't been so stupid, my sister would still be here." He shook his head. "I don't expect you to understand."

"You think I don't understand blame? If I hadn't been born, my mama might still be in Swans Landing and not stuck here. The humans back home might not be so afraid of the finfolk if my mother had never had me. Don't tell me about guilt, Callum. I've lived with it every day of my life."

"You can't blame yourself," he told me. "The actions of your parents don't make you guilty of anything."

I laughed. "Spare me the lectures when you've just insisted that you're a murderer because of an accident."

He dropped his head. "I have wished every day for the last five years that I could go back and change everything."

"You know what my grandma would say?" I asked.

He raised his eyebrows. "No. What?"

"If wishes were horses, beggars would ride," I said in my best Gale Mooring impersonation.

He blinked at me for a moment, then laughed. "I don't think I understand, but maybe your grandmother is a wise woman."

"She is," I said, sighing as I thought about her.

"Do you miss her?"

I nodded. "And I'm worried about her."

"Then we should go back to her," Callum said.

I raised my eyebrows. "We?" I asked.

"I brought you to Hether Blether and to Domnall," Callum said. "So maybe it's my duty to help get you safe again."

"How?" I asked. "You can't make that swim."

Callum frowned. "I'll figure out a way."

A tingle started up my arm, spreading throughout my body. When he reached over to cup my cheek in his hand, I closed my eyes, breathing in the scent of him.

His warm breath brushed across my lips and I opened my eyes again to find his face only inches away. He leaned forward, pressing his forehead against mine.

"I shouldn't want to kiss you," he said. "I shouldn't be allowed to feel something good after everything I've done."

"You want to kiss me?" I asked, my heart pounding against my chest.

"Very much."

I swallowed, staring back into his eyes. "I want you to kiss me," I whispered.

He trembled slightly as his mouth moved toward mine. The sound of birds and the ocean around us vanished when our lips met. I no longer felt the cold, wet earth beneath my feet. There was only Callum and me, and the feel of his arms pulling me into him as he kissed me deeper.

Chapter 26

Josh didn't say anything when Callum and I returned to the suite holding hands and for that I was grateful. This thing with Callum was new and strange and exciting and confusing all at once. I had spent my whole life convinced that Dylan Waverly was the person I was always meant to be with. From the time I was born, it was always Dylan and me.

Now, I wasn't sure of anything.

Later that day, I wanted to go see my mother. Josh and Callum and I had discussed quietly the idea of leaving as soon as possible. I refused to leave without Mama, but whether she could actually swim all the way back to Swans Landing was still the big question.

I sent word to Artair that I wanted to go to the peninsula, and I wasn't surprised when we arrived at the bay to find Domnall waiting with his sentry.

"No one invited you," I told the finfolk king.

He smiled, not looking at all bothered by my annoyed tone. "It is my duty to ensure your safety while crossing the bay," he said.

Callum scowled. "I can ensure her safety," he said. "Go back to the palace."

Domnall looked coolly at Callum. "Need I remind you that you do not issue orders here?"

Callum's glare deepened, but he said nothing as we all boarded the boat.

The extra weight in the boat made it sit low in the water, and the small waves lapping against the side sometimes splashed over, collecting at our feet. I could feel the tug of the change inside me as my feet soaked in the cold saltwater in the bottom of the boat, but it wasn't enough to force the transformation.

Mama sat at her desk again when I entered. Josh and Callum stood on either side of me, while I felt Domnall's presence in the doorway behind us. I gritted my teeth, ignoring the unwanted audience, and stepped across the room.

"Mama?" I asked softly.

She was drawing, her hand moving smoothly across the paper. It was a drawing of the Swans Landing lighthouse, rising above the beach where it stood near the northern end of the island. She had captured it with the eye of someone who had spent a lifetime looking at the lighthouse every day.

"Mama." I knelt next to her, putting a hand on her bony shoulder. She didn't flinch or move away. She didn't seem to even notice I was there "Do you want to go home?" I asked as quietly as I could so Domnall couldn't hear.

She kept drawing, her greasy hair falling over her shoulder and into her face. I pushed it back behind her ear, the way Grandma had always done for me. An overwhelming homesickness washed over me. I could see Grandma in Mama's face. I could hear her voice in my head, even smell her in the air around me.

I wanted to go home.

"Mama, we're going back to Swans Landing," I whispered "I'll take you home. I'll take you to Grandma. We have to swim and we'll be there"

Mama's thin lips cracked open, though she didn't look away from her drawing. "I have to go," she said.

I nodded. "Yes, we'll go."

"I have to find it," Mama said.

I blinked. "Find what?"

"I need it." A crease formed between her eyes and she frowned deeply. "I promised I would find it."

"What is it?" I asked gently. I hoped she wouldn't become agitated like before and shut down again.

"I need the key." Mama turned her head toward me, her eyes wide. "It will save us."

I had no idea what she was talking about, but she

looked on the verge of another breakdown, so I rubbed a hand over her head and nodded. "Okay. We'll find it, then we'll go home. I promise."

She sat back, looking satisfied. Then she turned her gaze toward the window. "I think I'll go swimming today," she said.

She was back in her own world inside her head. I stood, trying not to let out the sobs that were building inside me. How could I take her on a swim all the way across the ocean in this condition?

But how could I think about leaving her here?

"Are you all right?" Callum asked as I turned toward him.

I avoided his gaze, but nodded. "I'm fine. Let's go."

Domnall gave me a sympathetic smile. "I am sorry for your mother's condition," he said. "It is a shame to see someone who should be so healthy and in her prime like this."

"If you're so sorry about it, why haven't you done anything to help her?" I snapped as we left the cottage. Josh grabbed my arm, shooting me a warning look, but I shrugged him off.

"What would you have me do?" Domnall asked. "Your mother is beyond our help."

"Then let her go home," I said. "Don't keep her hidden here away from everyone else. Let me take her home and get her help."

"I told you, this is the effect the human world has on finfolk," Domnall said. "This is what will become of all of you if something is not done. I am only trying to help."

Callum stepped forward. "You only want to control everyone," he said. "You have no proof that the human world has done anything to anyone."

Domnall gestured toward the cottage. "Is that not proof enough for you?"

"Maybe you did something to her," Callum said. "I wouldn't put it past you. What methods did you use to try to get her talk that left her like this?"

My blood ran cold in my veins at Callum's words and the idea that Domnall might have tormented my mama for information about Swans Landing. I didn't want to think about her going through that, but it made sense. Why else would she be like that?

Domnall glared down at Callum. "You dare speak to your king in that tone?"

Callum didn't back down or break Domnall's gaze. "You know you are not my king."

Domnall stared back at him for a long moment, then stepped back. "Very well. Then I no longer feel compelled to give you my protection or services. Enjoy your walk back to the village."

Domnall's robe fluttered behind him as he swept across the grass and white sand to the shore where Artair waited. Domnall climbed into the boat and Artair picked up the oars. With a push, they were off, Artair rowing back toward the other side of the wide bay.

Josh shaded his eyes as he watched the boat move farther away from the shore. "He left us here," he said with a tone of disbelief.

"It isn't that bad," Callum said. "It will be a long walk, but we can manage." He shifted a little on his good leg, rubbing his thigh where the prosthetic met flesh under his robe.

"Are you sure you're up for it?" I asked.

"I'll be fine," Callum said, giving me a smile that didn't quite reach his eyes. "It certainly isn't the worst thing Domnall could do to me. I'm sorry you two are stuck walking with me."

"It's fine," Josh said. "We don't mind. And if you need help walking, let us know."

I sighed as I looked across the bay. "I'll be glad when we get back home. The finfolk homeland hasn't been anything like I expected."

"You are only seeing the ghost of what it used to be," Callum told me. "Imagine an island full of beautiful homes and finfolk everywhere, on the land and in the water." He gestured toward the bay. "There were once homes there, below the water. Finfolk used to travel often between the many vanishing islands."

"What happened to all of that?" Josh asked.

Callum shrugged. "Most of it had already faded into stories by the time I was born. One by one, the vanishing islands were found by humans and claimed as their land, destroying the magic that kept them hidden. Hether Blether is the last of our islands in existence. There was a disagreement long ago, between two groups of people, the ones who wanted to remain hidden and the ones who wanted to find a way to exist and survive in the human world." He raised his eyebrows at us. "One group left, hundreds of years ago and were never heard from again. Until now."

I frowned. "Do you think Domnall is right? Will Hether Blether die out if our people don't come back?"

Callum shook his head. "What's wrong with Hether Blether isn't the fault of your people. It's our own. Forcing a group of finfolk to leave the only home they know is not the answer."

"It's funny," Josh said. "Your story about Hether Blether sounds a lot like Swans Landing."

When I looked at Josh questioningly, he continued. "Everyone says Swans Landing was once a bustling vacation spot. Tourists came from all over to fish there or relax. Now hardly anyone comes anymore. People have left, both finfolk and human. If things stay the way they are, Swans Landing might die out too."

The wind that swept over the bay was icy and it stung my eyes and ears. I didn't like to think about the future Josh was predicting. If both Hether Blether and Swans Landing died out, what would become of the finfolk that were left?

"I thought there were some similarities between the two," Josh said, shrugging. He raised his eyebrows. "Ready? I hear it's a long walk."

Callum reached for my hand, entwining his fingers

with mine. "Ready," he said.

Chapter 27

"It will be a long swim," Callum said. "You're already at a disadvantage with me joining you."

I glared at him across the table in our suite. "I don't care. I'm not leaving without my mama."

"I agree with Sailor," Josh said. "We came so far to find her. We still have questions she hasn't yet answered. We need to take her home."

Callum sighed as he threw up his hands in frustration. "Are either of you thinking this through? The woman is daftie. Has she even been back in the water in the past sixteen years? Maybe Domnall did the same thing to her that he did to me. Maybe she can't change anymore."

"She's *not* crazy," I said. "She's sick. We have to take her home and get her help. Grandma will know what to do."

I wasn't sure my grandma could do anything for her, but I had to hold out hope that she would know. Gale Mooring always knew the right cure for everything.

"And what if the swim back only makes her condition worse?" Callum asked me quietly. "She left that place for a reason. What if being back there only brings back the memories she is trying to forget?"

I dug my fingernails into the wood, forcing myself not to cry at his words. I didn't want to think about that possibility. Right now, the only thing I could focus on was getting away from Hether Blether.

"We're taking her with us," Josh said, his tone stern, as if his decision settled the matter. "Even if I have to hold her hand the entire swim back, we'll get her home."

I cast a grateful look at Josh and he gave me a small smile in return. I knew he had his own selfish reasons for bringing my mama with us. He still wanted answers as to what happened the night our daddy died. But I was happy he took my side in this argument anyway.

"What do we do if she can't change?" Josh asked Callum. "Is there a way to reverse it?"

"I don't know of anyone ever reversing it," Callum said. "But I suppose it could be possible, if you sing the right song. It would take a lot of power to do. And she would need to be in the water to help force the change."

"Why don't we try it on you now?" I asked. "Then you could swim with us."

Callum shook his head. "It takes a lot more energy out of you than you think. I'm not going to let you use all your strength on me when you still have your mother to worry about. Besides, changing form wouldn't bring my leg back. The song can't regrow limbs. But I'm still finfolk. I won't drown, but I will be a lot slower than I used to be."

I hoped Callum was right, and he could survive such a long swim in human form.

"We'll go after sunset to get her," Callum decided. "The darkness will help hide us."

"What do we do until then?" Josh asked.

"We'll need supplies," Callum said. "Tools we can use. Knives, ropes."

"Food," I added, making a face. "Something other than fish."

"We don't have our waterproof bags anymore," Josh reminded me. "We'll have to be careful about what we can take in the water."

Callum nodded as he stood from the chair. "We should go back into town before the merchants close their wagons."

I raised my eyebrows. "Do you think you should go? I mean, after what happened last time..."

Callum's expression turned grim and he frowned. "You're right. I would only cause trouble. We don't need the extra scrutiny right now. The more we remain invisible, the better. You two go, I'll stay here."

He looked as if it pained him to stay behind, but it was for the best. We didn't want word to get back to Domnall that we were planning to leave, and Callum's presence in the village would only cause problems.

"We'll be back soon," I told him.

We slipped out of the palace, keeping a close watch for Domnall or his men. I expected Josh to ask the question I knew was burning on his tongue. But he walked silently beside me, his hands buried in the pockets of his hoodie, which he still refused to get rid of though it reeked of sweat and salt.

"Well?" I snapped finally.

"Well what?"

"Are you going to ask what's going on between Callum and me?"

Josh shrugged. "I can see what's going on with my own eyes."

"It's not...I don't..." I sighed. "It's complicated."

"How so?" Josh asked.

I kicked at a small stone in the path. "I like Callum, but..."

"But then there's Dylan waiting for you back home," Josh said.

I rolled my eyes. "He's not waiting for me. He probably doesn't even care if I never come back. We haven't pledged ourselves to each other or anything."

"But you and Dylan have a history together," Josh said. "And he might not be happy when you come home with a new finfolk."

I rubbed my temples. "Can we not talk about this right now?"

"You're the one who brought it up," Josh said. He paused and pointed toward the beach to our left. "There's Artair."

I made a face as I looked at the finfolk sentry, who stood along the edge of the water just where the surf washed up on the sand. The beach was empty except for him. He faced the water, his eyes shielded from the late afternoon sun. He lifted a hand and waved, and I scanned the water to see what had his attention.

Two heads bobbed not far from shore, one much smaller than the other. The woman in the water lifted her hand and waved to Artair, then she lifted the child at her side out of the water as a larger wave washed over them. The woman disappeared, but she held the child above the wave's surface as the little girl kicked her legs and splashed. Her laugh drifted across the beach toward us.

Once the woman had resurfaced, Artair turned away from the scene. His eyes caught mine, and his expression darkened into a deep scowl.

"Let's try to avoid him," I muttered to Josh.

Despite how late it was getting, there were still people walking around the village square when we arrived. Most of the vendor wagons sat in their usual spots, though the food wagons had only a few things left. Josh and I decided to split up so we could blend into the crowd a little easier on our own rather than together. Josh went in search of tools that could help us while I shopped for food.

We had brought a few things from the palace to trade, dishes and forks mostly. I managed to trade two forks for a bag to hold my purchases and then set about finding fruits and vegetables I thought could survive extended time underwater.

I was finishing up my shopping trip when a familiar figure stepped in front of me at the last wagon. I scowled up at Artair, who kept his usual neutral expression.

"Do you mind?"

"Why are you here?" he asked.

I waved my bag of fruit at him. "Shopping."

He narrowed his eyes. "Why were you spying on my family?"

I rolled my eyes. "We weren't spying on anyone, especially not you. I don't care what you do with your family. Frankly, I'm shocked you even have one."

I pushed past him and examined a display of strange yellow fruit I had never seen before. I felt his presence over my shoulder, though I refused to look at him.

"You should not have freed Callum," Artair told me. "He is a criminal. He committed crimes that are the worst a finfolk can do to his own kind."

"Callum told me everything. An accident doesn't make him a murderer."

"He planned to reveal our people to the humans," Artair said. "The actions of which resulted in another finfolk's death. He might as well have killed her with his own hand."

Now I turned to face him. "You people have a sick sense of justice. His sister dies by accident, and you think that justifies cutting off his leg and taking away his ability to be finfolk? What is wrong with you?"

But my words didn't seem to have any effect on Artair. "Callum gave up his right to be finfolk and swim as we do when he turned his back on his people."

"He was trying to help all of you," I said.

"He failed in his duties as protector of our people," Artair said. "He deserved to be stripped of everything—his ability to swim, his heritage, his title."

I blinked. "What are you talking about? What title?"

One corner of Artair's mouth quirked. "So he did not tell you everything. Callum was meant to sit on the throne that Domnall now occupies."

I took a step back. "What?" I asked, trying to make sense of this.

"Callum was meant to be king of the finfolk in Hether Blether."

I shook my head. "I don't believe you."

Artair inclined his head toward me. "Then I suggest you speak to Domnall and find out the truth about

Callum for yourself."

Chapter 28

Artair led me directly from the market to Domnall's suite in the palace. I was aware of the stares as I followed Artair past the merchant wagons. With his spear clasped in his hands, it looked like I was being taken away as a prisoner. I hoped Josh wouldn't hear about it and try to come rescue me.

I didn't want to talk to Domnall, but I needed to hear him tell me why he sat on the throne if Callum was supposed to be the finfolk leader. Mostly, I needed to know why Callum hadn't told me this himself.

My stomach twisted as I waited in the silent hall. Would Domnall even agree to see me after what had happened at the peninsula?

After a moment, Artair returned and gestured for me to follow.

Domnall waited in the den of his suite. The shutters over the windows were open to allow the ocean breeze into the room and the crystal prisms made rainbows dance on the walls.

"This is a surprise," Domnall said, standing as I stepped toward him. "To what do I owe the pleasure of this meeting?"

"Why isn't Callum king?" There was no need to make small talk. I only wanted to hear what he had to say and then I would return to my suite to prepare for our leaving.

Domnall raised his eyebrows. "Ah. Did Callum finally confess everything to you?"

I glared at his back as he turned toward the pitcher of water and cups on their usual table. "Callum told me what happened to his sister," I said. "And why he was banished. But I had to hear about this from Artair."

Domnall glanced at Artair, who still stood in the doorway. The guard bowed his head slightly and Domnall waved a hand at him. Artair stepped out of the room, pulling the door shut behind him.

"Artair may have overstepped his position a bit," Domnall said. "He should not concern himself with this."

"So then you tell me," I said. "Why are you here and not Callum?"

Domnall poured a cup of water and then offered it

to me. When I shook my head no, he took a sip and then returned to his chair. "Please sit."

"I'd rather stand," I told him.

"Callum was stripped of his birthright because of his actions five years ago," Domnall said. "In actuality, the person who was meant to sit on the finfolk throne was his sister, Pearl. As the oldest child of their parents, she became queen after their deaths. Callum was her heir only until she gave birth to her first child, which unfortunately, did not happen. She was still only a young woman when she died."

"And how do you fit into this story?"

"When Pearl died, the throne transferred to Callum automatically," Domnall said. "Callum was meant to be our king. But when he told us what had happened, how his actions had killed his sister...To take the life of another finfolk is the greatest sin we can commit. The person responsible must be stripped of all rights, even the right to be called finfolk. Callum lost his birthright. There were no other siblings the title could transfer to. No cousins close enough to his father's royal blood to have a legitimate claim. But there was me."

He took a sip of his water, then set the cup down. "Pearl was my wife."

My mouth dropped open. "You were married to Callum's sister?"

"Aye. I had been captain of the finfolk guard for many years. Pearl was under my care, and I watched over her as a faithful servant. We fell in love, and married only a year before..." Domnall cleared his throat. "Before she died. When Callum was stripped of his birthright, I was named king by request of the finfolk people."

"And then you cut off Callum's leg," I finished, crossing my arms. "Your own family."

Domnall frowned. "I gave the order for the punishment, aye. It is our custom. It is what we must do to protect ourselves."

"And going after my home, is that to protect yourselves?" I asked.

"To save my people, it is what I must do."

"What about the humans who live there? What do you plan to do to them?"

Domnall shrugged. "Humans are not my concern. They have done nothing for us except take our land. We lost the other islands long ago, and we're losing Hether Blether now. If the only way to fight back is to take the land that humans walk, then that is what I must do. I will rally the finfolk I find in the human world. They will see my side once they know the damage humans do to us. Once we unite all finfolk together again, we will be able to push the humans out of their land and rebuild the finfolk kingdom, stronger than it ever has been before."

I shook my head. "You don't know the humans. They'll fight back, and not all finfolk will be on your side."

He gave me a placating smile. "And you, wee one,

being raised so far outside of our world, do not know the power of the finfolk. Have you never heard the stories about us? About how we could convince human men and women to leave their homes, their families, for the chance to live a life with us? The finfolk song is more powerful than you know. We show the humans what they want most, and their will is easily bent."

I swallowed and gripped the edge of the chair in front of me to help steady myself. I didn't want to believe Domnall's words, but he sounded convincing even now. "You can't do that. The people of Swans Landing haven't done anything to you."

Domnall's eyes flashed. "But humans have. They are an infection on this world and I intend to put an end to their taint."

"Why?" I asked. "Why not bring back the finfolk who want to leave and then live here away from them?"

He narrowed his eyes as he studied me. "Why do you concern yourself so much with the humans? Why do you care what happens to them?"

"I don't. I care about my home." I turned to leave. "Thank you for speaking with me. Callum and Josh will be waiting for my return."

As I reached the door, a low hum started behind me. The air around the edges of my vision sparkled with gold light. I stopped, my hand frozen in midair above the doorknob. The humming grew louder, the sound vibrating through me and tickling the hairs all along my arms.

I heard a voice next to me, a whisper in my ear. "Child, don't make me come after you." Grandma. Her voice so clear in my head. A shape began to form and I could smell her salty scent. My legs trembled, my knees almost giving away.

I clenched my teeth and forced myself not to look. I couldn't let Domnall see that his song had any effect on me. He would know I was part human.

But it was hard to resist. The two parts of me battled inside my body. The finfolk side told me to run and pretend not to notice. But the human side begged for a glimpse of Grandma, who I knew I would see standing next to me.

Sweat trickled down my back between my shoulder blades. I bit my tongue so hard I tasted blood. I still carried the bag of fruit and I clenched my fist around the fabric, squeezing as hard as I could until the muscles in my arm burned.

Slowly, my other hand reached the doorknob. With painful movements, my eyes locked on the wall in front of me, I pulled the door open and then walked out, leaving Domnall still singing and the vision of Grandma caught in the air behind me.

* * *

Callum looked up from the knife he was sharpening on a rock when I burst into our suite. He leaped from his seat when he saw me, grimacing when he put weight on his wooden prosthetic. I had run across the palace once I'd left Domnall's suite and I was out of breath. My mind was swirling inside my head like a hurricane, thoughts bumping into each other as I tried to make sense of them.

"Are you all right?" Callum asked, standing quickly. "Did something—"

"Why didn't you tell me you're supposed to be king?"

Callum froze, his face paling so the freckles on his cheeks stood out. "Who told you about that?"

"I spoke with Domnall." I swallowed, trying to settle churning sensation in my stomach. "He told me everything. Your sister was queen. And Domnall is your brother-in-law."

Callum's eyes darkened. "*Was* my brother-in-law. The man he is now is not the same one who married my sister."

"Why didn't you tell me?" I asked. "You told me your sister died and that you were banished for it, but you never told me she was the finfolk queen! You never mentioned you are supposed to be king."

"I'm not!" Callum shouted. He bent over the table, pressing his fists into the wood. "I'm not king. I was never supposed to be king. Pearl was queen. Her children should have succeeded her, not me. But never she had a chance to give birth to an heir." His body slumped, his shoulders shaking. "Because of me."

228

"So the title transferred to you," I pointed out. "You're royal blood, Callum. You don't think that at least deserved a small mention, somewhere in between kissing me and telling me about your childhood here?"

Callum shook his head. "I have no title. Not anymore. I lost my right to every claim when my actions killed my sister. I am not finfolk, but I'm not human either. I am nothing, which is exactly what I deserve to be."

I crossed my arms. "You should have told me."

His green eyes shone with the sheen of tears. "And what difference would it have made if I had?"

"You kept this secret from me," I told him, my voice shaking a little. "How can I be sure you're not keeping other things from me too? How do I know you're the one I should trust and not Domnall? How can I be sure of anything now?"

He straightened, his body tense. The muscles in his neck twitched and his hands clenched into fists at his sides. "I told you all along you should be careful who you trust. Maybe that includes me too."

"Callum—"

But he walked past me, his wooden leg thumping on the hard wooden floor. He pushed open the heavy door and stomped out, letting it slam shut behind him.

Chapter 29

I tossed and turned all night, but sleep never came. I was already up, curled in one of the chairs next to the window, when Josh woke the next morning.

"Did Callum come back?" he asked.

I shook my head. "I don't think so." I hadn't heard him return, though I had listened for the sound of his wooden leg thumping across the floor all night long.

Josh had returned to the suite after Callum had left. He'd been angry that I had left the square without him, but he forgot about that when I told him what had happened with Callum.

"I don't want to hear that I was too hard on him," I said, shooting a glare at Josh.

He raised his hands in surrender. "I wasn't going to say anything."

He had said enough the night before. He didn't seem to understand why I felt so betrayed by Callum not telling me about his heritage. But how else was I supposed to feel? I thought I had known who Callum was, but now I realized how little I knew about him.

And yet, I still held my breath, listening for the sound of his footsteps outside the door.

But there was nothing except the rhythmic whoosh of the water under the suite.

"We should go find him," Josh said, as if he could read my thoughts.

"Can we trust him?" I asked. "Maybe we shouldn't trust anyone except each other. These people aren't like us."

"He's our friend," Josh pointed out. "He helped us get here and kept us safe."

A knock on the door startled me and I leaped from my chair, heart pounding against my ribs.

But when the door opened, it was Domnall and not Callum. My shoulders sagged as I tried to steady my pulse.

"I came to invite you to have breakfast with me," Domnall said with a pleasant smile.

I narrowed my eyes. "Why?" Domnall had not invited us to breakfast with him during our entire stay. As Artair had mentioned, Domnall usually ate his meals alone in his suite and had only eaten dinner with us once.

"I will be leaving Hether Blether tomorrow," Domnall told us. "I am looking forward to the journey to your land. I thought it would be nice to have one last breakfast together, a toast to good fortune on the trip."

Josh and I exchanged glances. We needed to leave Hether Blether before Domnall did. Time was running out.

"Okay," Josh said, surprising me with his acceptance. "Give us a moment to get dressed and...presentable."

He sounded so formal and awkward, but this place was different from the world we'd always known.

Domnall nodded. "Very well, I will expect you in the dining hall shortly."

He turned to leave, but I called out, "Wait!"

When Domnall stopped and looked back at me, his eyebrows raised, I said, "Do you...Have you seen Callum?"

Only a slight expression of surprise passed across Domnall's face. "Callum? I thought you knew. He left Hether Blether last night."

My stomach plummeted to my toes. "He what?"

Josh stepped to my side. "When did he leave?"

Domnall waved a hand vaguely. "He came to me last night and requested a boat. He vowed to abide by his banishment and leave the island for good." He shrugged, giving me an apologetic look. "I assumed you knew he was going."

I shook my head. Callum was gone? Without even saying good-bye?

"Why would he leave?" I asked.

Domnall held out his hands, palms up. "I do not know. He seemed rather insistent on leaving right away, however. I must admit I was surprised to see him go, but perhaps he realized his error in returning here."

Josh put his arm around my shoulder, pulling me close to him. "Thanks for letting us know," he said. "We'll be at breakfast soon."

Domnall gave us one last smile and then left, closing the door behind him.

"I can't go to breakfast," I told Josh. If I ate anything, the queasy feeling in my stomach might make me throw up.

"We're not going to breakfast," Josh said. "We're leaving."

"We are?"

Josh's expression was grim. "If you're right and Domnall suspects we're not fully finfolk, this place is too dangerous for us, especially now that Callum is gone. We need to get out of here as soon as possible."

Josh was right, as always. Callum had made his decision and apparently, it didn't involve me. I pushed aside my sorrow over Callum, but another problem still remained.

"What about my mama?" I asked.

"Grab what things you can." Josh walked over to

the cabinet where he had hidden the bag of tools he'd packed last night. He pulled out a small knife and belted it to his waist, then handed another one to me. "We're going to get her now."

We had no boat to take us to the peninsula, so we ran along the shoreline, our feet slipping in the soft sand. My lungs felt as if they would burst at the effort of our run, but we couldn't stop. The sooner we were swimming away from here, the better.

I didn't knock before entering the cottage with the lily-carved door. Mama sat at her desk again, bent over her drawings.

"Mama," I said, trying to catch my breath. "Come on, we're going home."

Mama didn't look up, but continued scratching at the paper with her charcoal.

"Grab some of her things," I told Josh. "Whatever you think will be useful."

As Josh headed toward the tables to inspect the items scattered there, I went to my mother and put a hand on her arm.

"Mama," I said softly. "I've come to take you back to Swans Landing. We need to hurry."

She had a smudge of charcoal on her chin and it made her look like a child. "Home?" she asked.

I nodded. "Yes, home. We're going home, but we have to leave right now."

She shook her head, bending back over her drawing. "I need to find the key."

"Mama." I fought against the impatience rising inside me. "Please. I can't leave without you."

I glanced at the paper in front of her. She was drawing Moody's Variety Store. It was perfectly detailed, as if she were looking at the image right in front of her.

I pointed at the drawing. "Do you remember this store?"

She nodded. "Daddy's store," she said.

Tears stung my eyes. "Yes, it is. Your daddy still works there. So does your mama. My grandparents. We have to go home to help them. Something bad is coming to Swans Landing, and if we don't get there in time, Grandaddy won't be able to fight back. His store might not be there anymore. *He* might not be there."

She looked at me with glassy blue eyes. "Daddy?" she asked.

"We have to go help him," I said. "We have to go now."

"We need the key," she told me.

She let me pull her to her feet and I led her out of the cottage. Josh followed, carrying the bags of tools and food. Mama had that glazed look on her face, already beginning to slip back into her thoughts. I wished I could get a reaction from her again. I wished she would think Josh was his dad. Something. Anything other than this blank stare.

We ran toward the water's edge, where white waves crashed against rocks in the surf. As we stepped onto the wet sand, Mama pulled back, yanking her arm free of my grip.

"No!" she shrieked and ran away from the water.

I chased after her, grabbing her arm and pulling her to a stop. She fought back against me, but she was so thin and small I could easily hold her in place despite her thrashing.

"No!" she shrieked again, her voice echoing into the distance. "I need the key!"

"Mama!" I said. "Mama, it's okay! We're going home."

"He told me to get the key."

"What key?" Josh asked, kneeling next to us.

Mama's eyes grew wide. "Oliver," she panted, reaching toward him. "I tried to find it. I went where you told me to go."

"That's good," Josh said, rubbing his hand over hers. "Where is the key? What is it?"

"The *key*," she said.

I gasped, my gaze darting to Josh. "The key," I repeated. "What if she means the key Callum had? The one that brought us here."

Josh looked as if the pieces had clicked in his head too. "Ms. Mooring," he said gently. "Do you mean the finfolk key?"

She nodded, still breathing heavily. "We need the key."

Josh gave me a helpless look. "But where is it? What happened to it after we got here?"

"Domnall has it," I said. "In his suite. I saw it there, in a drawer."

Josh groaned, rolling his head back. "How are we supposed to get it without him noticing?"

We were very late for breakfast by this point. Maybe Domnall had given up waiting for us. Maybe he had already realized we were gone. It would be a risk to go back to the palace now, but something about Mama's insistence on getting the key made me reluctant to leave without it. What did she know about the key that I didn't?

"We'll have to split up," I said. "You distract Domnall while I take Mama with me to get the key."

Josh shook his head. "No way."

"It's the only option we have, Josh," I told him. "We'll meet you at the beach under our suite. Distract Domnall for a few minutes, that'll be long enough."

Josh let out a deep breath. "I don't like this," he said grimly. "But let's get it over with."

Chapter 30

"Shh," I whispered to Mama as we slipped along the hall that led to Domnall's suite.

But I didn't have to say anything. She followed behind me, her bony hand clasped in mine, as I led us toward the double doors. We had spotted Domnall near the dining hall with Artair, and Josh had gone off to distract them while Mama and I went to get the key. My gaze darted back and forth as we moved, but there was no one else nearby. The only sound was our feet shuffling across the sandy floor.

I held my breath as I turned the iron knob, hoping it wasn't locked. The door creaked open and I slipped inside, pulling Mama along with me.

The suite was empty, the shutters over the windows closed tightly. Even the door in the floor over the beach was closed, as were the doors leading to the bedrooms. The main room was dark and shadowy without the light streaming in the windows. I shivered in the cool air.

"Over here," I told Mama, whose gaze was unfocused. I made my way around the furniture to the table where I had seen Domnall pull the key from a drawer. I bumped into a chair in the dim light, banging my knee.

I bit my lip to hold back a curse and then paused, waiting to see if anyone outside the room had heard the thump. I thought I heard a soft shuffling and I turned my head, straining to figure out where it came from. To my right? There were two doors on one wall, which I assumed led to bedrooms like in my suite.

My pulse pounded in my ears. *Relax,* I told myself. *Domnall isn't here.*

I tiptoed toward the table and pulled the drawer open.

There was no key.

The only thing inside the drawer was a small gold locket, engraved with seashells. I picked it up, letting the locket swing back and forth on the chain.

"Where's the key?" I asked out loud.

I heard a shuffling again and I spun around, facing the doors.

"Mama," I said, reaching for her hand. "Stay with

me."

She took the locket from my hand and then slipped it over her head, humming softly to herself as I pulled her across the room. I pulled open every drawer and cabinet I could find, working my way around the room as the minutes ticked by. I had told Josh I only needed five minutes. How long had we been here already?

I pulled open a cabinet in a large wooden wardrobe and spotted a silver box on a shelf. I eyed the box for a moment, then reached up and took it down from the shelf.

When I opened the lid, there it was. The twisted piece of black metal.

"The key," Mama said, looking down at the box.

I nodded. "This is what you came to find, isn't it? Did Oliver tell you to find this?"

Mama smiled. "Oliver..."

A thump behind one of the doors to my right made me jump. I dropped the silver box, letting it crash to the floor at my feet. I tucked the key into the belt of my robe and then placed my fingertips on the knife Josh had given me.

"Sailor?" a familiar voice called, muffled through the closed door. "Sailor, is that you?"

"Callum!" I rushed toward the door and turned the knob, but it wouldn't open. I pounded on the wood. "Callum! What are you doing here?"

"Domnall locked me in," Callum said. "Last night, when I came to talk to him after I left the suite."

"He told us you had left the island," I said. Tears blurred my vision. He wasn't gone. He had been here the whole time, and I had almost left without him.

"I would never do that," Callum said. "I'm sorry I didn't tell you about my title. But I would never leave you here."

I pressed my palm to the door, as if I could feel him through it. "We have to get you out of there."

"Domnall has a key somewhere," Callum said. "I saw it before he closed the door and locked me in."

I scrambled around the room, searching the drawers and cabinets I had already looked through. But I couldn't find any keys other than the one that led us to Hether Blether. It didn't look as though it would fit the old fashioned lock on the door.

"Let me try something," I said, kneeling in front of the door, my knife in hand. I stuck the tip into the keyhole. It was a small, slender knife, the right size to hide in someone's hand. A girly knife, I thought with a smirk. Of course Josh would keep the big knives for himself.

I glanced over my shoulder to make sure Mama hadn't run off. She stood near a small bronze statue of a mermaid on a table, running her fingers over the tail. "We'll be going soon, Mama," I told her. "I have to get this door open."

"Sailor," Callum said through the door, "you should get out of here. Go before Domnall catches you."

"No." I dug the knife into the lock hard, blinking

241

away a bead of sweat that fell into my eye. "Not without you."

Something inside the lock clicked. The door swung open and Callum stood there, looking down at me with amazement in his eyes. He wrapped his arms around me, pulling me into a tight embrace and lifting me off the ground.

"This is a touching reunion," said a voice behind me.

Callum dropped me back to my feet. My stomach plummeted as I faced Domnall, Artair, and two other guards, their spears sharpened to fierce points. One of them held Josh's hands behind his back, a spear pointed at his throat.

The door to the beach was right behind us. A few steps and I could pull it open and jump down into the water below.

But Mama stood on the other side of the room, still admiring the small mermaid. And Domnall's men had Josh.

Callum stepped in front of me. "Let them go."

"I cannot do that," Domnall said. "I have caught her in the act of helping a condemned criminal escape. That makes her as guilty as you."

Josh's eyes met mine. I saw something there, a look of defiance before he acted.

I stepped forward, calling out, "No—"

But Josh lunged at the guard holding him, shoving his shoulder into the man's chest. Taken by surprise, the guard fell backward, dropping his spear and sending it rolling across the floor.

Josh started toward us, but Artair swung his spear at him. The blunt end whacked Josh in the side, making him stagger backward, coughing and gasping. Josh collected himself and lunged at Artair again, only narrowly avoiding being pierced by the end of his spear.

I turned away from the sight, not wanting to see Josh hurt or killed. It would be my fault if he died here, four thousand miles away from Swans Landing. He needed to go home. I didn't even mind if he went straight to Mara, as long as he was safe.

Callum pushed me away from him as he too lunged into the fight.

I stumbled before catching myself on the edge of a chair. Mama still stood by the statue. I had to get her out of here. I had to get her back home.

I started toward her. "Mama," I called. "We have to go."

I didn't notice the other guard who had broken past Callum and Josh. I didn't hear him over the sounds of the fight behind me. But the sudden impact of his spear against the back of my head cracked loud inside my own ears. The world went black for a moment and I stumbled to the floor.

Mama's humming grew loud in my head, causing golden sparks to burst at the corners of my eyes. I squeezed my eyes shut, silently begging my head to stop spinning so I could focus.

I rolled over, opening my eyes slowly, to face the sharp end of a spear pointed directly at my chest.

Chapter 31

I raised my arms over my face, as if flesh and bone could protect me from the sharp end of the spear. I squeezed my eyes shut, holding back the scream building inside me.

A grunt made my eyes snap back open. The guard wavered a moment, then fell, collapsing onto the floor next to me. In his place stood my mother, her hair wild and whipping around her head, the bronze mermaid clutched in her hands. A trickle of blood oozed from the back of the guard's scalp and puddled on the floor.

Mama's gaze moved toward me and her face paled. "Sailor," she said.

I leaped to my feet, throwing my arms around her

tiny frame. "Mama," I whispered, hugging her tight.

"Sailor," she said again. When I pulled back, I could see the blankness was already returning to her eyes. The clarity that had existed in them was so brief, so quickly erased.

I choked back a sob. "Mama, no, stay with me. Please."

"She will never be well," said a voice at my side. Domnall stood over us, the lines in his face deep. Josh and Callum struggled with Artair and the other guard. Domnall's cheek was bruised across the jagged scar. He hadn't escaped the fight unharmed. "As long as humans taint the earth, your mother will never be well."

"I'm taking her home," I told him. "Let us go. You got what you want, you don't need us anymore."

Domnall laughed. "Do you think I trust you? You will return to warn your people about me. I will not let you leave this island until I have what I want."

I stepped away from him, pushing my mother behind me. "We want to go home."

Domnall moved toward us. "Whether you stay or go, I will still be free to do what I want. But you will be less trouble to me if you stay here."

I grabbed the knife from my belt, holding it awkwardly toward Domnall. I had never held anyone at knife point before and felt a bit silly now. But I tried to hold my hand steady and glared at Domnall.

"Wee girls should not play with sharp objects,"

Domnall growled. He extended his hand toward me. "Hand it over before you hurt yourself."

I swiped at the air between us. "Leave us alone or else I'll hurt you. I swear."

He tilted his head, narrowing his eyes. "I do not think you will. Have you forgotten the consequences of harming another finfolk? Do you want to end up like your beloved Callum? Could you endure a life with one leg?"

I pushed Mama backward toward the door in the floor. I could feel her shaking, and I prayed she wasn't about to have another panic attack. *Hold on, Mama,* I said silently. *We're almost there.* Once we were in the water, we could change and swim away.

I couldn't leave Josh and Callum, but I didn't see how I could save them and Mama and myself.

"We can talk about this, Sailor," Domnall said. "You could be happy here. You would be where you belong. You could have everything you have ever wanted."

My gaze had been so focused on Domnall that I didn't notice the shape moving behind him until Callum suddenly rose up, like a part of the shadows. Behind him, the second sentry was out cold like the first.

"Your fight isn't with her," Callum said, his nostrils flared.

"My fight is not with you either," Domnall growled. "You are nothing to me or to Hether Blether."

"I'm the rightful king," Callum said. "You are the imposter."

Domnall laughed. "You gave up your rights when you killed my wife."

"You are unfit to be king. I'm taking my claim back."

"You have already been charged with treason once, Callum," Domnall said. "You should not push your luck a second time." He stepped backward, closer to me. Callum followed, his fists curled at his sides and his muscles tensed.

"Let them go. You don't need them."

"Oh, but I do," Domnall said. "I still have use for them. Perhaps they might be useful in my dealings with their people."

"Pearl didn't marry the man you are now," Callum told him. "She wouldn't have loved you like this."

Domnall's face turned red. "Do not tell me what Pearl would have wanted! You took her from me. *You* killed her!"

With a swiftness I hadn't seen before, Domnall lunged at me, ripping the knife from my still outstretched hand. He pushed me backward, sending me crashing into Mama and we fell to the floor in a tangle of limbs.

I sat up, pushing the hair out of my eyes, as Callum lunged at Domnall. The finfolk king turned around to meet him, swinging his arm.

Callum's gasp echoed through the room, roaring

over the sound of Artair and Josh struggling on the floor. He doubled over, the blood draining from his face and turning his skin white.

Domnall stepped away, letting Callum fall to the ground. He still clutched the knife in his hand, though now it dripped with bright red blood.

It took a moment for me to realize the piercing noise in my ears was my own scream.

Callum rolled over on the floor, his hands pressed to the blooming red stain on his robe.

Domnall stepped back, his steely gaze locked on Callum. "I am king here," he said in solemn voice. "And that is the way it will remain."

Artair and Josh had frozen in mid-battle, and now they both stared at Callum. A dark red pool stained the floor next to him.

Domnall glanced at his unconscious men, then jerked his head at Artair.

"Come," he barked. "We must prepare for the journey."

Artair rose to his feet, but his gaze was still locked on Callum's prone figure. He appeared to wobble a moment as a grimace passed across his face. But then he held his shoulders back and the serious expression overtook his face once again. He turned and followed Domnall out of the room.

I crawled across the floor to Callum. He was so still, his eyes looking unfocused at the ceiling overhead. Was he dead? Had I led him to his death after everything he'd already been through?

I let out a breath when he finally blinked, slowly.

"Callum," I said, leaning over him.

He turned his head to look at me and lifted one hand from his side. "Sailor," he said in a hoarse voice.

Tears fell down my cheeks, dripping onto his hand. "I'm sorry. I'm so sorry."

"It is all right," he told me. "This is what should have happened to me five years ago."

"No." The word choked me and I leaned over, burying my face into his shoulder. I pressed my ear to his chest, listening to his heartbeat. As long as I heard that steady beat, I could hope he would be okay.

But even as I listened, I could hear it slowing.

If only we were in Swans Landing. Grandma would know what to do. Grandma could fix anything.

As I lay there with Callum, I became aware of a roar underneath me and an ache deep in my bones. The ocean. We were on top of the door that opened to the beach below. I could smell the salt in the air and feel the whisper of the water calling to me. I wanted to shed my human form and become finfolk, letting my body remake itself.

I sat up, gasping.

"Josh," I said. He stood with Mama, holding her hand gently as they looked down at us. Mama was eerily quiet and still, her eyes wide and focused on Callum. "We have to get Callum into the water."

"He'll bleed to death," Josh said.

I shook my head. "We can use the song to heal him. The body undergoes a rebirth during the change from human to finfolk. It remakes itself."

I had tried to sing the song before and had failed, but I had to try again. I couldn't sit here and let Callum die in this place.

"Josh, please," I said. "I need help getting him into the water. We have to try."

"Okay," Josh said at last. He glanced at my mother. "What about—"

"Mama," I said, stretching out my hand. "Mama, remember? It's me, Sailor. We're going home."

I hoped somewhere inside her was still the clarity I had seen moments ago. A tiny spark was all I needed.

Josh helped me move Callum off the door and then we pulled it open. It was high tide and the water foamed and crashed under us.

Mama looked at me, then Callum, and then at the water below the opening. Finally, she looked at Josh standing next to her.

"Oliver?" she asked.

Josh hesitated, then nodded. "Yes, it's Oliver. Follow me, Coral. Let's swim."

"You can't swim," she told him.

"Yes, I can," Josh assured her. "Follow me and we can swim back home. Together."

Mama studied him a moment longer. Then she smiled and jumped through the opening into the crashing surf below.

251

Chapter 32

Josh and I swam with Callum between us, moving farther away from the shore and into the waves. Mama followed close behind, not speaking, but at least she was moving with us.

The change I had tried to hold back as long as I could took over and I sank under the water, releasing a gasp of pain in a stream of bubbles. Bones popped and moved, skin stretched and tore, ripping away to reveal red and silver scales. My body shed its human form and became the other me, renewed and revitalized with the salt water I inhaled.

When I resurfaced, I found Josh and Mama also bobbing among the water. They too had changed.

Mama held her hands up in front of her face, as if she expected them to grow scales as well.

But I didn't have time to feel relief at the fact that Mama could still change form. Callum bobbed in the water next to me and he moaned, his face contorted into pain. I hoped the blood he was releasing wouldn't attract curious sea life. I didn't want to find out what it was that had injured the finfolk woman we'd seen on the beach that day.

"We have to sing like the finfolk on the beach did," I said to Josh. "Use both the earth and the water songs."

Josh didn't look confident, but he nodded.

I closed my eyes, leaning my mouth close to Callum's ear, and I began to hum, pulling the vibrations from deep within me. It was hard, but I squeezed my eyes shut and focused all my thoughts on the two songs. Josh's voice joined mine and he moved close, helping me hold Callum up in the water.

I became aware of another voice in our song, an alto I had never heard before. I lifted my head and found my mother near Callum's side. She helped hold him stretched out across the surface of the water, running one hand over the gaping wound in his side. Salty tears burned my eyes. I had dreamed of hearing her song my whole life.

Callum thrashed slightly, his eyes squeezed shut. He was still pale, much too pale. He kicked one leg, the one with the prosthetic. I reached down to unhook it from his leg, holding onto it to keep it from floating away.

Callum arched his back and cried out, and we sang louder. I pressed my forehead against his, focusing on the vibrations of the earth and the sea around me. My pulse throbbed in my head, my body already feeling exhausted with the effort. *Please, please work.* It had to work. I had nothing else I could do for him.

When he stopped thrashing, I lifted my head. His eyes were closed, but his chest moved up and down as he panted. He still lay on the surface of the water among the undulating waves around us.

But now he had changed.

He had only half a tail where his leg ended. The left side of his tail was there, but the right side ended in a scarred edge where the rest of his leg once was. His scales were brilliant green, like an emerald, and his half of a tail fin spread out in a translucent blue-green web.

I turned him onto his side, my hands clutching at the area where the knife had gone in. Where there had once been blood oozing out, now only freckled skin with a light line marking it remained.

Callum opened his eyes, blinking. His gaze found mine and he smiled slowly.

"Hello," he said.

"Hey," I answered, laughing as relief swept over me. I wrapped my arms around his shoulders and pressed my lips to his, tasting the salt on his mouth.

We sank under the water for a moment, our tails entwining. Already I could feel the warmth returning to his body despite the cold water.

We resurfaced, shaking water out of our eyes.

"Well," Callum said, "I should almost die more often."

"Don't you dare," I told him.

Chapter 33

The sun peeked through the hazy clouds that hung low in the sky when I opened my eyes. Morning dawned, and birds were already flying over the ocean in search of breakfast. Water gurgled in my ears as I lay drifting on the surface, bobbing among the rippling waves.

With a flick of my red-scaled tail, I dove deep into the water, then twisted around and broke back through the surface, arcing gracefully. The ocean enveloped me as I slipped back in, wrapping me with the familiar song I felt deep inside me.

"Show off," a voice said when I resurfaced, blinking water out of my eyes.

I turned, and couldn't help the grin that stretched

across my face at the sight of him. He looked more alive than he had in all the time I'd known him. I knew that under the water, his tail bore the scars of what had been done to him, as it would for the rest of his life. But I didn't care. He was alive, and he was truly finfolk once again.

"Well," I said with a shrug, "when you feel like diving, you gotta do it."

Callum swam closer to me, reaching out to grab my hand. I let him pull me toward him, until our noses were only inches apart. His half of a tail fin brushed against mine, sending a tingle through my body.

"And when I feel like doing this—" He pressed his lips to mine in a kiss that made me feel weak all over and we slipped below the surface for a moment before coming up again. Then he pulled back and winked. "I have to do it."

"Do you have to do that first thing in the morning?" Josh wrinkled his nose at us from where he tread water nearby. Mama stayed close to his side, as she had done since we'd left Hether Blether two days ago. Most of the time she stayed quiet, just following along next to us. Other times, she thought Josh was his daddy and would talk about random memories, though she never mentioned the night he died. I wasn't sure yet if she even remembered that night at all, and I didn't want to risk having her break down in the middle of the ocean by asking those questions.

Besides, we had other things on our minds right

then. Domnall and his men had certainly left Hether Blether by now, so we swam for as long as we could each day, stopping for only a few hours of rest when absolutely necessary. For all we knew, Domnall was right behind us, using whatever methods he had to track us through the water.

There was no land anywhere in sight. The ocean stretched on into the horizon all around, like land had disappeared completely. It would be another long, hard swim.

The key hung heavy against my waist, still tucked into the belt of my robe. We could return to Hether Blether any time we wanted as long as we had it.

But all I wanted was to see another island on the other side of the ocean.

Josh yawned, rubbing sleep from his eyes. "Everyone ready?" he asked.

I nodded, looking from him to Callum and then to my mother. "Let's go home."

About the Author

Most days, Shana Norris still feels like she's stuck at sixteen, which is probably why she enjoys writing about teens. She always wanted to be a mermaid and fell in love with the Outer Banks during a gray late winter years ago. She lives in a small town in eastern North Carolina with her husband and small zoo of pets, which currently includes two dogs and five cats.

You can visit Shana online and learn more about her books at www.shananorris.com.

Other books by Shana Norris:
Troy High
Overtime: A Troy High Novella
Something to Blog About
The Boyfriend Thief
The Rules of You and Me
The Swans Landing Series

Swans Landing Series

Don't miss the rest of the books about the finfolk of Swans Landing!

Along the Outer Banks of North Carolina lies a small island that holds secrets as big as the ocean. A race of beings called finfolk walk among the humans, only changing into their mermaid form while swimming. For centuries, the humans and finfolk happily shared the island and the surrounding waters.

But that has changed.

Surfacing (Swans Landing #1)
Sixteen-year-old Mara Westray has just lost her mother, and now, being shipped off to live with the father she doesn't know is not how she imagined grieving. But from the moment she steps off the ferry, nothing is as ordinary as it looks.

Submerging (Swans Landing #2)
Sixteen years ago, Sailor Mooring's mother dove into the Atlantic Ocean and was never seen again. Now, Sailor is following her mother's long swim to find answers to the questions that have haunted her life: Why did her mother leave? And what really happened the night Sailor's father died?

Shifting (Swans Landing #2.5)
Dylan Waverly has lived his entire life on the tiny island of Swans Landing with his best friend Sailor Mooring at his side. But now Sailor has left, and no one knows if she'll ever return. Dylan remains stuck in a half-life between land and sea on an island that is slowly dying.

Surrendering (Swans Landing #3)
Josh Canavan swam an entire ocean in search of the truth about what happened the night his father died. Now he's made the journey back in order to save the people and the island he loves.

www.ingramcontent.com/pod-product-compliance
Lightning Source LLC
Chambersburg PA
CBHW071135170626
46809CB00002B/636